EFFEMINATE
EARTH

JULIA ELIZABETH FLOWERS

This book is a work of fiction. Any references to historical events, real people, or real locales are used fictitiously. Other names, characters, places, and incidents are products of the author's imagination, and any resemblance to actual events, locales, or people, living or dead, is entirely coincidental.

978-0-9974959-0-4 (paperback)
978-0-9974959-2-8 (hardcover)
978-0-9974959-1-1 (eBook)

Credits

Book cover design and interior layout by
Ellie Bockert Augsburger of Creative Digital Studios.
www.CreativeDigitalStudios.com
Editing by Susanne Carlisle

Waving White Flag: © denisismagilov / Dollar Photo Club Handsome athletic young man isolated on white background: © Subbotina Anna / Dollar Photo Club Earthquake: © isoga / Dollar Photo Club

Dedicated to Mary Kathryn Johnson, without whom this book would not exist.

And to my father, the strongest person I know.

PREFACE

The NannyBot 650, shining and gleaming in all its titanium glory, looked nearly lifelike after its latest update. The bot was the newest version of the in-home assistant for women who wanted help taking care of children while their mothers were away at work. It also assisted women who chose natural birth instead of SGI, Scientifically Generated Incubation. Almost every mother owned one to rear their children while they were away, even if they didn't choose the natural birth option.

When Sarah Williams had told her doctor that she wanted a natural birth, the doctor had been beyond surprised. Almost no one chose that now that they had the option of continuing daily life with no disturbances for 40 weeks while the SGI Department manufactured your baby. While doctors agreed that natural birth was potentially better for the baby, they also agreed SGI was more convenient for the working parent.

Despite Sarah's position in the SGI Department, she wanted a natural birth. She had done a lot of research before making this decision. Having access to SGI files that a lot of people didn't, meant that Sarah knew exactly what went on in her department.

Nine months after artificial insemination, Sarah's baby girl was due. The NannyBot 650 helped prep Sarah with sterilized equipment and the best painkillers money could buy.

The moment contractions started, NannyBot 650 gave Sarah the pain meds and waited. Once she was fully dilated, NannyBot just pulled the baby out; no pushing, no pain, no discomfort necessary.

"Look at your beautiful baby girl!" the robotic voice cheered, laying the small, wrinkly, pink potato on Sarah's chest.

Instantly she knew something was different. This was no girl. Sarah had read about a few cases like this where the scientists who generated the semen made a miscalculation and out came a boy. That's what the Department of Male Eradication was for. While rare and unlikely, sometimes boys were born too...and they couldn't have that after all the work they'd put into getting rid of men.

But Sarah knew from the moment that she laid eyes on her child that he was important, special. She couldn't let the government get him. She loved him too much to lose him. Her heart rate increased tenfold as she stared at the metallic robot that would surely want to do an APGAR, an ancient medical process that had survived through BME, Before Male Eradication.

The NannyBot reached out to take the baby and preform it's assessments, but Sarah quickly handed it a wadded up blanket instead. Knowing it wouldn't stay fooled for long, she darted off the birthing table and hid the baby in a grocery panel in the kitchen.

The NannyBot moved slowly, but it was highly intelligent for a robot. When it caught up to Sarah in the kitchen, the blinking lights that it used as eyes seemed to be narrowed at her.

"Where is the child?" it droned.

Sarah knew there was no way to shut it off. She was sure that it had already signaled the Department of Male Eradication. There was only one way to defeat it: Sarah had to outwit it. She had to confuse it, and she had to do so before the Eradicators arrived.

"What child?" Sarah stalled, trying to think of a way to overcome its artificial intelligence.

The NannyBot made a sharp beeping noise and suddenly began searching through the kitchen: under tables, in wall panels, everywhere it could process. The Bot used something between an x-ray, echolocation, and laser image processing to see.

Sarah cleared her throat, gaining the bot's attention. She had no idea what she was doing, but she knew she had to do it quickly while she had its undivided attention. What was one thing artificial intelligence couldn't understand? The answer sprung into Sarah's mind: emotions.

Sarah knew little of love as it was discouraged strongly in Femater, but she knew that whatever she felt for that little boy was something awfully close to it. She filled her mind with thoughts of him, thoughts of his warmth against her skin, his eyes staring at her inquisitively, eyes that matched her own. And then, knowing the NannyBot could read minds through touch using the electrical impulses of the brain, Sarah surged forward, wrapping her arms around the bot's cold, smooth surface.

The metal instantly began heating up under her touch and she wanted to yank her body away from it, but Sarah willed herself to stay where she was until finally the NannyBot activated its self-shutoff feature due to emotional overload.

Sarah let go and walked around to the backside of the bot to remove its memory chip. She smashed it under her heel after taking it out and then turned her attention back to the baby which had began to cry.

Sarah picked him up and cradled him in her arms, cooing soothingly. She rocked back and forth, walking to the hallway where her secret panel was hidden. The previous tenant of the home had installed it in fear of the frequent wars. As far as Sarah could tell, it had never actually been used.

Sarah walked down the staircase that had been revealed by the sliding panel and set the baby in the secret basement, then hurried back upstairs, trying to ignore the pain from too much movement directly after birth.

Before the government officials could arrive, Sarah logged onto her secure government account on her HoloNet and changed her record to say SGI instead of natural birth. Nobody would expect anything; the doctor had put her on bedrest at around four months, before she really began showing. She certainly hadn't told anyone the reason for her leave of absence. That would have been crazy; her boss wouldn't have supported her due to her choice of natural birth.

Next she disposed of the sheets and all the equipment used during birth. Just as Sarah was deleting the security footage and replacing it with a looped video of Sarah sitting at her HoloNet, there were three loud raps on the front door.

"Open," Sarah said in a level voice.

The door swung open to reveal four tall women. The first of the four had light brown hair. She stepped forward and said, "Your NannyBot 650 has reported the birth of a male. You know what we are here for."

"Yes, yes," Sarah agreed, trying to sound exasperated. "It is defective. I've been down for SGI for about eight months."

The first woman, Jane, Sarah read off of her name tag, turned to her partner who was holding the HoloNet and whispered to her. The lady holding the HoloNet, Laura, gave a few swipes and nodded. "It says here that Sarah Williams of SGI Department ordered her SGI baby a little over eight months ago."

"Thank you, Laura," Grace, another of the four women, said. "Sorry for the trouble, Sarah. We'll dispose of the faulty NannyBot for you."

"Thank you, Grace," Sarah agreed with a nod. "As long as you're here, I'd also like you to take me off of the waiting list for a baby. My department is coming out with some updates soon and I'd like to wait for those."

Jane nodded and whispered to Laura again who swiped a few more times on her HoloNet. "Sorry for the inconvenience," Jane reiterated.

Sarah gave another nod and the four women left the house. She began to ponder all the illegal things she had done within the past hour and whether or not it was worth it, but before her mind could coalesce on this train of thought, the child began wailing again and Sarah rushed over to pacify him.

She hummed softly under her breath, rocking back and forth slightly as he gripped her finger, slowly drifting off to sleep.

CHAPTER 1

Abel swung his legs back and forth as he waited for his mother to return. She had said that she would bring Abel more things to do to pass the time, but Abel was getting sick of all these "time-passers". Passing time until what? The only thing Abel ever got to do was pass time. Read, draw, write, sleep, eat, learn, and his mother's regimen of exercise to keep him healthy and "sane". Nothing that made too much noise and definitely nothing that involved leaving his room. What was the point of it all? Why should he live if there was nothing of importance to his life? Nothing was going to change and Abel was sick of it.

His mother had three rules: never leave the basement, don't attract attention, and never under any circumstances let anyone see him.

Apparently being an unauthorized birth was a Big Deal.

When he was about ten he asked his mom what being an unauthorized birth meant. She answered with: "It means that you," she paused to poke his stomach, "are very special."

Abel didn't feel special. He felt bored. And now he knew the truth anyway. He was illegal, undocumented. In a world of perfect records and order, he wasn't.

Abel had learned about everything out there, but he'd never actually experienced it: grass, wind, sunshine, HoloNets, Chancellor Mia, the government, *grass*. All of which he knew, but none of which he *knew*.

Abel rapped his fingers gently on the desk in front of him. A news holo sat on the desk with moving pictures, animations, self-scrolling articles, and immersive holograms that "brought the news to you!" As he stared blankly at the screen, a holo of a street played. Some report about a family that had found a piece of space rock in their back yard. A grainy picture of the family flashed onto the screen, the man with his arm wrapped around the woman, and the woman with one hand on each of their two kids' shoulders.... Nothing that truly interested Abel. Why should he care when none of it actually affected him?

From above Abel heard the front door open and close and his mother's voice filled the house.

"No. That report needs to be turned in by Friday so that Chancellor Mia can review it." Pause. "Yes, yes. I don't care what it takes. I was appointed Head of SGI and therefore I make the decisions. I have to go. Yeah. I know."

Abel figured that she was talking on her HoloCom. She wouldn't come down until she ended the call; three-dimensional immersion meant that whoever she was talking to could see the entire room like they were actually there. Not that he would actually know.

The only things Abel had ever seen were the four walls that contained him and the contents of his room. Off-white peeling paint, no decorations, the small, sliding panel at the far end of his room the led to his tiny bathroom. The other end of the room housed his desk that was made of some sort of metal that had long ago lost its shine. It was the only furniture he had besides his bed and a little dresser that held all his clothes that his mother had made for him.

His mother opened the secret reinforced panel and slid in to Abel's room. Her caramel hair was tied up in a neat bun and her murky, green eyes looked tired from a long day of work. It amazed Abel how composed she was at all times. He had never seen her upset or angry or even happy or excited. Sarah Williams tended to stay placated and calm.

Abel, however, had the opposite personality. He was often brash and could be easily persuaded from one emotion to another. And the older he got, the more irresponsible he tended to be. Not purposely. He was just far too restrained for his personality type. Just last year he had gotten in trouble because he was blasting music while Sarah wasn't home. She had managed to convince everyone that her HoloMuse had broken and needed to be replaced. Abel had gotten a month of no time-passers and extra schooling.

Sarah neatly sat next to Abel and took his large hand in her two small ones. "Abel, I have good news."

"I get to go outside?" Abel asked excitedly.

"Well, not really. They've come out with a holographic simulation device, so you can make your room look like whatever you want: a grassy meadow, a rocky canyon, even the big city! Isn't that great?"

Abel felt himself deflate slightly. "Yeah...great."

Maybe he would have been enthused about this a few years ago, but now he was just tired of it. Abel had tried nearly everything and yet still nothing soothed the burning urge to have a purpose. He had given up fighting it. Sometimes, he realized, nature made you a certain way and it was best to embrace it.

He ran a hand through his messy black hair which his mother immediately tried to pat down. "You need a haircut again."

Abel rolled his eyes. "You say that every day."

"Well, that's because no matter how short it gets, it's still unruly. I think you do it on purpose," Sarah accused with a small smile.

It was true. His one way of rebellion was his hair. It drove his mother crazy to see it messy and out of control so that's exactly what he did. He made sure that his hair was always as wild as possible.

Abel just shrugged in response to his mother.

Sarah sighed and handed Abel the small cube that was in her pocket. "The HSD." Abel took it and set it on his desk next to the news holo which was now flashing a video of Chancellor Mia smiling and giving some speech. "Did you do your schoolwork for today?"

Abel affirmed and began to mess with the small cube. His mom let out another sigh. "I'm going to go make dinner. We're having roast."

Abel just nodded and his mother shook her head slightly before standing and leaving Abel again.

The worst thing about being underground all day, every day was that you had no concept of time. Even with the clocks littered around Abel's messy room, he could never understand time. He slept sometimes all day, got hungry at the oddest hours, and couldn't fall asleep at all sometimes.

Abel shook his head and set the holographic sim device back on his desk. He didn't want the simulation, he wanted the real thing. And he knew that seeing it would only make him long to go outside even more. He couldn't risk that. Sometimes the urge was so strong to just sneak upstairs and poke his head out of the front door.

It couldn't be that dangerous, right?

But he knew that he never would, because while he wanted to with all of his being, Abel would never risk it with all the things his mother had driven into his head about the dangers to not only himself but his mom as well.

He couldn't put his own mother's life on the line.

A few minutes later Sarah came back down, carrying a steaming plate of roast with potatoes and carrots. Abel's mouth watered at the smell of the surely succulent meat. He almost didn't care that it was nearly completely manufactured in a laboratory. Almost. But the nearly brown carrots curbed his ravenous hunger and made his previously watering mouth wrinkle with disgust.

"I know it's your favorite and since today is a special day, I thought we'd celebrate!"

Special day? Abel was drawing a blank. He stared at his mom with a perplexed expression.

"It's your birthday," she reminded. "You're eighteen today."

Abel was astounded. How can you not know it's your own birthday? That was how bad his concept of time was. One day blurred into the next until they were all one.

"I made cake," Abel's mom sang.

"Chocolate?" asked Abel.

Sarah nodded with the hint of a grin. Abel smiled at his mother, but on the inside he felt depressed. Eighteen years of prison and eighty-two more to go. So much to look forward to.

CHAPTER 2

Sarah had to work all day the next day, leaving Abel unattended in his little basement room with nothing to do. He was sitting on his bed, trying to focus on reading his history holo. But his mind kept wandering and his eyes wouldn't focus on the flat sheet of glass that was portraying BME lifestyle. His mom would never tell him what BME meant, but Abel knew it had something to do with measuring time periods.

He finally gave up on his schoolwork and was putting it down when he heard it: an ear-splitting scream of pure terror. Abel's hairs stood on end. What was going on? Was everyone okay?

Another screech rang out clearly through the walls and down into the secret room.

He had to help! He couldn't let whoever it was get hurt. But that meant having to leave his room. And leaving his room meant certain death.

No! Abel couldn't be selfish like that. All he had to do was sneak out and check if the girl was okay.

Abel took a deep breath and tried to stabilize his ragged breathing. This was what he'd always wanted, so why was he so terrified?

Sarah had left several hours prior for work, so he knew that he was home alone. He carefully mounted the stairs and pushed the buttons on the security panel that he had seen his mother press so many times before, causing the door to slide open. And then he faced a problem. Abel realized that he didn't know where any of the rooms were.

He walked down a hallway and found himself in what he thought was the kitchen. Deciding to take a left from there, he found himself in a large open room with minimal decorations. The walls were bright white as was all the furniture. And it smelled sterile. Like no human had ever set foot in it.

At the very back of the room were two windows on either side of a steel, swinging door. Abel walked over to it and hesitated one last time. What if he was too late? Then the third screech pierced his ears, willing him to plunge out into the vast unknown of his front yard.

When he opened the front door, the first thing he noticed was the brightness. It was blinding and disorienting and Abel almost cried out in surprise. Letting his eyes adjust, he surveyed his surroundings. The biggest difference was all of the noise. He was so used to silence that it was deafening to hear all the different commotions: birds singing, wind blowing through the trees, the crackle of gravel beneath his feet, shifting and throwing him off balance. There was a road in front of him and the street was lined with houses that were all identical to one another. In front of each house was a patch of...grass! Abel ran forward and bent down, feeling the grass with his fingers. It wasn't at all like he had imagined! The grass was slightly poky and made his hand itch after he drew it away. The vibrant green carpet was deceiving in looks, for it looked like a soft rug.

Feeling slightly disappointed at the discovery, Abel sighed and straightened back up. A light breeze was blowing and it felt amazing. Abel was used to the stagnant, stuffy air of the basement, but this air was fresh and crisp with a cool whip to it. The vibrant colors varied such with the dull ones of the basement that Abel was almost blinded.

As soon as his body had adjusted to the weird and unusual sights, sounds, and smells, he began surveying the area for whomever had screamed.

Off to the right in the distance, he could make out the figure of a short woman with her back facing him. It was unusual to see a girl shorter than 5'7 anymore. Most were somewhere between that and 6'2 from what Abel understood. His mom was always talking about her unusual height of 5'5. He towered over Sarah at a whopping 6'4, but this girl seemed even shorter. Maybe it was a child.

In front of the person was some robotic thing that towered over her threateningly and seemed to have a hold on her arm. Abel's heart pounded and his body seemed to move of its own accord; the next thing he knew he was yanking the girl away so forcefully that she landed on her butt with an "oomph".

Upon closer inspection, Abel saw that it was indeed a robot. A big, scary, menacing robot that made him want to run right back into his basement and never come out. Instead of fingers, it had long claw-like knives and it had some sort of needle protruding from its abdomen that Abel definitely didn't want to discover the purpose of.

All he knew was that he had to get it away from the girl. Glancing back, Abel saw two things. One: the girl was *not* a child. And two: she was only semiconscious.

He tried to formulate a plan, but his mind seemed to have stopped. The robot lunged forward and Abel dodged sluggishly, not expecting the sudden attack. Luckily, he managed to get out of the way in time without getting caught by the razor talons. Unluckily, his body slammed into a large, artificial oak tree.

A groan escaped his lips and he used the tree to support himself, pushing his forearm against it. The sun glared into his face off of the bot's shiny chest. And that's when the idea hit him.

Abel could tell that this wasn't a government-produced machine which meant someone had built it either illegally or bought it illegally. The robot was already moving towards him again.

Abel darted down the side of the street, brushing against the well-trimmed bushes. He could hear the robot behind him clicking and whirring, driving him to keep moving.

He was so thankful in that moment for the robotics class that his mother had made him take. He had read about how most nongovernment-made robots were built from scraps of other bots, making them inferior and the part that tended to be the worst was the locomotive center as it was the hardest to find and the easiest to mess up.

He could already feel himself running out of breath from running at full speed for so long, but he could also smell smoke. Just a little longer. He pumped his legs harder for the final stretch and just as he thought he was going to either collapse or pass out, he heard a loud clang behind him.

Abel halted and double over, placing his hands on his knees and panting so loudly that it echoed. When he had slowed his breathing enough to not die, he righted himself and walked over to the robot with jelly legs.

He touched the steaming and smoking metal and instantly jerked his hand away from the burning heat. Not having any way to access the memory chip panel, he kicked the back of its head repetitively until the thin, cheap aluminum caved in, revealing the innards of the robots brain. Jumbled wires and boxes and things dominated the space, but in the very center was a little round orb. Abel grabbed it and placed it into his pocket. It was the memory chip orb. Some robots, instead of just having a chip, had a chip orb which could also function as a control center, video storage, and hacking abilities that allowed it to control simple, nearby electronic devices.

He turned his attention back to the girl who was now several yards away. Abel jogged over to check on her; she was now sitting up and seemed mostly alert.

Her long, blonde hair hung loosely around her shoulders instead of being tied up in a bun. Instead of a skirt, she was wearing a pair of ripped up jeans and instead of a blouse, she wore a t-shirt and a leather jacket.

When she saw him, her eyebrows scrunched together.

"Hey!" she called out. "Are you the one that saved me?"

Abel was still a little ways away and realized that she couldn't tell he was unauthorized. How would she know that? She couldn't know that...right?

"I—uh—I...." Abel cleared his throat before continuing, "I am."

"Thank you."

"You-you're welcome." He was debating whether to get closer or not. He had to check if she was okay, but he also figured he really shouldn't interact with too many people. But how would she know he was unauthorized?

In the end, his conscience won over and he continued walking towards her.

"Are you okay?" he asked, noticing a tear in the arm of her jacket where blood was seeping out.

She didn't answer. Instead, her mouth hung open and she blinked up at him.

He was so screwed. Something stirred in the pit of Abel's stomach that reminded him quite of when he had the flu. Something in this girl's eyes told Abel that she *knew*.

Deciding to abort mission, Abel turned around and headed back in the direction of his house.

"Wait!" she exclaimed, jumping up grabbing Abel's arm as he tried to walk away. Her eyes widened slightly. "Your arms! They're like tree trunks!"

Abel's eyes widened. He thought this an odd thing to say, but she looked so perplexed that he felt panicked. He was *so* screwed. "I—"

Abel squirmed slightly under her analyzing gaze. Her bright blue eyes seemed to paralyze not only his body, but his brain too.

His palms began to sweat again.

The girl's light blue eyes widened incredibly and she began stuttering. "You-you-you're a...a *boy*! Oh my word! You...."

Abel also thought that this was a weird thing to say because *obviously* he was a boy. But her voice was loud and echoing and he knew that sooner or later she was going to attract attention.

So screwed.

CHAPTER 3

Abel slapped his hand over the girl's mouth. "Shush! You're going to get me killed!"

She tried to say something through Abel's hand, but it came out more like, "Or uh buoy?"

"Promise me you won't shout," Abel demanded.

She nodded with eyes still saucers. Abel removed his hand and held the girl by her shoulders. "I want you to forget you ever saw me. I want you to promise me that you won't tell anyone."

The girl was too stunned to speak. Her mouth was agape and she didn't move for quite some time. "So this is what a guy looks like! I've only seen a few pictures from our history holos, but they're really unpleasant. You don't look anything like that!" Abel frowned in confusion, but shook his head, deciding that now was not the time to be questioning this girl's odd babbling.

"Listen, I really need to go before I'm seen...again. But first I need you to promise you won't tell anyone. That would be like murdering me."

She nodded. Abel could tell her surprise was wearing off and being replaced by intrigue. She circled him a few times, inspecting what he looked like, Abel supposed.

"You're a lot taller than me," she noted. "And stronger and just larger in general, but you don't...you don't have...*curves*...."

Abel scratched the back of his neck awkwardly. "I, uh, don't really have time to explain the differences in male anatomy." *You should know anyway*, he thought to himself. "I have to...get home."

The girl nodded. "I'll help you," she decided. A look of determination crossed her face, replacing the expression of shock mixed with inquisition.

"No," Abel denied. "I can't involve you any further. It would be a danger to me and to you."

"You don't seem like a vicious killer," she mused, more to herself than to Abel. Why would she say that? Were most unauthorized people dangerous? And that brought him back to the question: how did she *know*? "I'll help you," she repeated louder.

Abel didn't answer. Instead he was reminded of why he came over. "Are you okay?"

The girl seemed shocked by this and then slightly embarrassed. "I'm fine."

"Are you sure you aren't hurt?"

The girl nodded. "Just a few scratches," she assured.

"What was that all about?" Abel inquired, forgetting momentarily that he should probably get going.

She laughed uncomfortably. "It was just some stupid prank."

"A prank to kill you?" he exclaimed incredulously.

"Listen, I don't want to talk about it."

Abel shrugged, hearing the finality in her tone.

"Do you know how to get home?" she asked switching the subject.

Abel began to answer, but then his eyes swept the street lined with identical house and the words died on his lips. He realized that he had no idea which one was his.

The girl smirked knowingly. "I'll help you."

Abel was about to object again, but decided that she was probably his only hope to get back to his basement.

"Fine, but I, uh, have a couple of rules. No talking about...*you know*. No touching me in any way. And absolutely no snitching."

She nodded. "Do you know your address?"

Abel had never bothered to learn it because it had never been important. He shook his head.

"Well, which way did you come from?"

Abel pointed and Harley nodded again. "This shouldn't be too hard," Harley said. "Each house is programmed to recognize its owners' DNA. Who's your mother?"

Abel hesitated. This could get Sarah in big trouble. He glanced at the expression on her face and he knew he could trust her. "Sarah Williams."

She busted out laughing. "How ironic! Did you, perchance, hug her this morning?"

Abel raised his eyebrow but nodded. This girl was weird. The girl inspected his shirt, running her hands over his shoulder blades and down his spine. Abel blushed and shuddered slightly. "I said no touching!"

"Aha!" the girl exclaimed. She retracted her hands and walked back around to face Abel. Between her forefinger and thumb she held a long caramel colored hair. "About how far down the street did you start?"

"About here."

She shrugged and walked over to the front door of the house in front of them. She pressed a button next to the doorknob and a little tray popped out. The girl delicately place the hair on the tray and pushed it back in. "Sarah Williams," a robotic voice announced. "Welcome home."

Abel grinned. "Thanks."

The girl was grinning too. "Welcome."

Abel was about to walk inside when she grabbed him again. "I never got your name."

"Abel," he informed.

"Harley Haim," she said, sticking out her hand.

Abel stared at her hand, perplexed. He glanced from her face to her hand a few times before she laughed and grabbed his hand, shaking it up and down. Abel tilted his head to the side with knitted eyebrows.

"It's called a handshake," Harley explained. "You do it when you meet someone."

"Why?'

"I don't really know," Harley said with a shrug. "Because society says so."

"I gotta go," Abel said awkwardly, pointing towards the house.

Harley nodded. "I'll delete the security footage behind you."

Abel walked inside and shut the door behind himself. He carefully trotted downstairs and hid himself back in his stuffy basement with his mind racing. As he hid the memory chip orb, he thought of nothing but Harley. She was...different. Not that Abel knew much about the normal, but there was just something about her that felt different. And Abel liked that. He liked that she was willing to help him instead of report him and he liked that she dressed differently than most women from what he understood.

Her words rang in Abel's head as he tried to fall asleep, keeping him awake, staring at the ceiling and replaying the day's events in his head.

CHAPTER 4

Abel awoke to the sound of his mother coming downstairs. "You didn't eat dinner last night," she commented casually.

Abel shrugged, not meeting his mother's eyes. "I fell asleep."

Sarah nodded. "I brought you breakfast before I head to work."

Abel nodded with his eyes still glued to his bedsheets. He had the oddest combination of emotions: excitement and guilt, happy and scared. He took the plate with steaming waffles from his mother. "See you after work." Abel said.

His mom nodded and left the room, glancing back once more before she ascended the stairs. Abel knew that he couldn't leave again; last time had been too risky and dangerous. His sense of adventure was killing him to get outside again though. And Harley. He couldn't stop thinking about the girl who was willing to help the boy who was supposed to be dead. Half of him wasn't worried at all, only longing to see her again. The other half—perhaps the more logical half—was fretting and debating about whether she'd turn him in or not. It was tearing him apart.

Abel took a bite of his breakfast when he heard someone knocking around upstairs. His mother had already left, so unless she had forgotten something, it wasn't her. Abel's heart pounded and his blood was roaring in his ears. Adrenaline pumped through his legs as he heard the panel sliding open. He couldn't think, he couldn't move. His door slowly creaked open revealing a girl with long blonde curls and huge blue eyes. Harley.

Abel sighed in relief. "How...how did you get in here?"

Harley's mouth split into a huge grin. "I found you!"

"But how?"

Harley grinned even wider. "It was pretty easy. I skipped school and waited for your mom to leave for work. I remembered where you live from yesterday. I may or may not have stolen a second hair yesterday while I was deleting the security footage. I figured you wouldn't be out in the open, so I looked for some sort of secret room and I noticed that in the hall a square of the wall didn't quite match the rest in color, so I slid it open and a security panel was revealed. I managed to hack into it and sure enough..." She gestured to Abel, "...here you are!"

"This is really dangerous, you know."

Harley's grin didn't falter. "I know! It's exciting, isn't it?" She let out a laugh.

Her laugh was contagious and Abel found himself smiling in spite of himself. "What are you doing here though? I can promise you that there isn't anything interesting here."

"You're here," Harley countered.

Abel felt his cheeks heat up. "My point exactly."

Harley shook her head with a smile. "I want to know everything about you, about this situation."

Abel shrugged and began telling her his tale, beginning with the story of the mistake birth that he'd heard a million times. He worked his way through his childhood and his mother's rules, the way he was kept secret, how he'd never stepped foot out of his room until yesterday, his schooling, time-passers, and his mother's latest gift. His story was a bit stilted and awkward; he hadn't talked to anyone besides his mother and he definitely hadn't talked about his life to anyone.

Harley was a good listener though. She didn't interrupt the entire time and reacted appropriately to every dramatic part of his story, gasping, tutting, shaking her head, smiling, laughing, and she even cried a little bit when it got really depressing.

Once he had finished, Harley told him about herself and the outside world. Abel learned that Harley wasn't well liked due to her inquisitive personality, tomboyish ways, and knack for questioning authority. She had a sister named Hillary who was the golden girl in everyone's eyes and Harley was always being compared to her. Harley was seventeen and had always been on-the-fence towards the government's views.

"...and then Hillary," she paused to make a noise in the back of her throat, "went and *told* the instructor that I had taken off my dress and was walking around in my tank top and shorts."

"What's wrong with that?" Abel wondered aloud.

"Well, promotion ceremonies aren't exactly meant for tank tops and shorts. It's a formal event. But I *hated* it. We were all wearing matching, gray dresses and they itched like hell. And I was *eleven*. But did that matter? Nope! As soon as the instructor found out, I was punished, forced to wear the hideous monstrosity, not to mention publicly humiliated. And Hillary got a pat on the back and a reward."

She continued ranting for a little longer about different things. When Harley had finished explaining about her life, she cleared her throat and said, "Anyway, I want learn about males. You obviously aren't what they try to portray you as, you aren't the bane of existence, a savage killer, a rapist, or rampaging warlord, but what are you really like? What makes you any different from me? You have a soul, a beating heart, a personality, hopes and dreams, so what makes you different?"

Abel frowned. "I'm not sure I understand what you mean."

"What do you mean you don't understand?"

Abel furrowed his brow deeper in confusion. "You keep talking about males as if they're a foreign species, an alien or something."

Harley gasped. "You don't know," she said almost to herself.

"What don't I know?" Abel asked, feeling dread building up inside of him.

"How could you not know?" she muttered. "Abel, grab me your HoloNet."

Wanting nothing more than to press the point, Abel hesitantly stood and walked over to his desk, grabbing his HoloNet and handing it to Harley. "What's going on?" Abel demanded.

Harley ignored him and tapped vigorously away on the HoloNet. Another gasp escaped from her slightly parted lips. "This would've taken quite the ruse.... The programming and blocks set up on this thing.... Wow, this is complicated coding."

"Harley?" Abel prompted tentatively as his stomach tied itself in knots and heat rose up his neck.

"The censorship..."

"Harley," Abel repeated louder.

Finally, Harley looked up and met Abel's eyes, concern written all over her face. "Abel, maybe you should sit down."

"Harley, you're really starting to freak me out!" Abel said, taking a seat at his desk chair.

"Abel, I don't know how to tell you this..."

"Just spit it out!" Abel finally burst out.

"Abel...males are extinct. You're the last one in existence...and you weren't even supposed to be born."

Just like that, Abel's world shattered into a billion pieces.

CHAPTER 5

Abel wasn't sure how he made it to the toilet but he was retching into it as his mind swirled. He couldn't think, he couldn't breathe. His whole life—no, his whole existence—was a lie. How could he be the only male? How could he not know? Why would his mother lie to him? Anger spiked through all the confusion.

He was vaguely aware of a presence behind him. Harley.

Her voice sounded fuzzy and faraway. He couldn't make out her words.

Abel flopped over to the side of the commode and tried to stabilize his breathing. This wasn't possible. It was a joke. It had to be.

But he knew it wasn't.

Harley was kneeling next to him with a hand laid carefully on his shoulder. For once he didn't object.

"I don't understand," Abel muttered, burying his face in his hands.

"I know. Come on, let's get you back to your room and I'll try to explain the best I can," Harley whispered soothingly.

Harley took Abel's arm and led him back to his bed, and delicately placed herself next to him after he had dropped down onto the mattress.

Harley's entire demeanor had changed. Gone was the wild, smiling girl and replacing her was a serious, empathetic person. "I know this is really difficult to absorb and really confusing. That HoloNet you have is completely blocked and censored. That news holo you were looking at is the same video they play in history museum in the BME exhibit. BME meaning Before Male Eradication. I don't know how your mom managed to pull off that ruse, but it was flawless."

"How the story's told is a long time ago when the world had dipped to one of its lowest points, succumbing to war and violence and chaos, scientists linked all the blame somehow to men and slowly began weeding out the male species until there were none left. It was a gradual process. They segregated men into all male communities. First they killed any male babies that were born, then they led raids on the all-male communities. They slaughtered them like pigs. And without the restrictions and distractions of men, the females were freed to solve what little problems remained and to expand scientifically and stuff like that.

"This is today's actual news holo," Harley finished while handing Abel the Net.

Replacing the article about the family that found the space rock from a few days ago were flashing headlines: elections for heads of departments, new sustainable energy break-through, treaty between Femater and Masculum, Department of Male Eradication releases new security information regarding the DME vs Masculum case, Chancellor Mia addresses nation about terrorist threats. A wave of dizziness crashed into Abel again. It was too much. It was all too much.

Harley looked like she was at a loss as to what to do and say as she sat stiffly at the edge of Abel's bed. "I'm sorry," she said finally, as though it was all her fault.

He couldn't bring himself to respond to her.

"Maybe I'll just go," Harley said. "I know that this is a lot to process. I'll let you think on this and let it sink in and I'll come back tomorrow."

Abel turned his head to the side slightly as Harley left, and then the brooding started.

CHAPTER 6

Abel sat on his bed all night thinking. He was the last male, and he was a mistake. He was never supposed to exist. He was supposed to be dead. His mother had lied to him. She had tricked him. But why?

His mind always circled back to the whys.

The time between when Harley left and when his mother came home was enough to prepare him for the inevitable confrontation. Every time he thought of his mom red hot anger speared through his mind making him forget everything else.

Finally, after what seemed like forever, he heard the door open upstairs and his mom puttering around the house a little. Then the metallic click/whoosh noise of the panel echoed down the stairs and vibrated around inside Abel's head.

She was coming.

Click clack, click clack. Click clack, click clack.

His mom's heels reverberated in the small stairway. All the questions drained out of his head and were replaced by rage.

Abel jumped up just as his mother entered his room. She wasn't particularly paying attention to him, seeming kind of distracted.

She instantly began talking. "Hey, sweetie. How was your day? Work was so tiresome."

Abel cut her off by clearing his throat and stepping in front of her so that she had to look at him. He tried to form a coherent thought but all that came out was, "Why?"

Sarah frowned in confusion. "Why what, love?"

The anger that had been building up inside of him finally broke loose with a mighty growl. "You know why what. Why did you lie to me? Why did you block my HoloNet and set up this little-little hoax? Last male in existence? Didn't you think I'd find out eventually?"

His mother's face fell and she ran her hand over her eyes. "How did you find out about that?"

"That doesn't matter right now! Don't turn this around on me!" Abel yelled, balling his fists.

"Not so loud," Sarah hushed, glancing over her shoulder.

"Not so loud? *Not so loud*?!" Abel bellowed, waving his arms around. "That's all you have to say? Not so loud?!"

"It isn't my fault!" Sarah yelled, surprising Abel. "Don't you dare go and blame me for this. Not for one second, mister. I did this to protect you."

Abel glared at his mother. "Protect me?" he spat. "How could this have possibly protected me?"

Sarah narrowed her own eyes. "What was I supposed to say when you asked to go outside? 'Sorry, Abel. If you walk outside everyone will experiment on you on, torture you, kill you and then do the same to Mommy.' No! I couldn't tell you that. You would've been scared out of your wits for your entire life. Not to mention how isolating it would've been—more so than already."

Her excuses flew right over Abel's head because of his seething. "I can't believe that you not only lied to me for eighteen years, but you planned on continuing to lie to me for the rest of my god awful life. What was your plan, Mom? Let me rot down here for all of eternity? What about after you died? Who would've 'protected' me then? Did you even have a plan?"

"I had a plan—*have* a plan," she amended. "Times are changing."

Abel didn't know what she meant by that and he didn't really care. "Just get out!" he screamed, stabbing his finger towards the exit. "Just leave!"

His mom recoiled, but then a defeated look clouded her face and she sullenly retreated back upstairs. After she had left, Abel collapsed on his bed facedown and closed his eyes. Sleep didn't come that night. Never before had he fought with his mom and all the new information clouded his brain, eluding him from rest.

CHAPTER 7

Harley's breath was short as she crouched in a pokey bush in front of the boy's house. *Abel,* she scolded herself, *his name is Abel.*

Just as Harley had begun to reposition herself to get more comfortable, the door slid open, causing her heart to race. She tried to settle her ragged puffing. Out walked a woman who was fairly short. Definitely taller than Harley, but still short. Her light, honey hair was pulled back into a tight, pristine bun. Harley had seen her before, but never up close.

Sarah Williams. She had just been elected head of her department.

Harley was surprised by how age-worn and tired she looked, but then supposed that if she had been hiding Abel for eighteen years, that could lead to some undue stress.

Sarah cast her gaze in the direction of Harley's bush, and Harley sucked in a gulp of air. Her murky green eyes swept across the shrubbery and Harley's heart leapt into her throat. Was she about to get caught by Abel's mother?

Just when Harley thought Sarah was about to walk over, she turned and elegantly strode down the street, disappearing against the early morning horizon.

Breathing a sigh of relief, Harley stood and approached the door cautiously. Stopping in the driveway to compose herself, she took a few deep breathes, smoothed her shirt, and brushed off a few stray leaves. But then the click-clack of heals filled her ears again, reverberating around inside her brain.

Harley's heart skyrocketed again, thumping against her ribcage.

She sped to the roadside, so she wasn't standing directly in front of Sarah's house. And not a moment too soon. Sarah had returned and was heading straight towards Harley. At first she didn't seem to notice Harley, but after glancing up, Sarah did a double-take and beelined directly to her.

"What're you doing here?" Sarah said in a rushed voice. "School started twenty minutes ago."

"I, uh," Harley fumbled, "I took a wrong turn and now I'm lost."

"Oh," Sarah sighed, sounding relieved. "Well, if you continue down this road, take a right and then another left, it should lead you directly to the backside of the school."

"Okay, thanks," Harley answered with a small smile, turning around and beginning to walk away.

Harley glanced over her shoulder to see that Sarah was also leaving again. When she was sure that Sarah wouldn't see, Harley ducked behind a large tree and hid until she was sure that Sarah was gone.

Then she resumed her stare-down with the front door. It wasn't that hard. He was waiting for her. She smoothed her shirt again and with a final deep breath she plunged into the dark house to find the mysterious boy.

Just as Harley had promised, she came back the next day. Abel had been left breakfast by his mother, but he had ignored her. When his door opened a second time, he knew it was Harley.

When she got down all of the stairs, she sat next to him on his bed and just stared at the wall for a few seconds. "Listen, I'm really sorry," Harley said finally. "You shouldn't have found out the way you did."

"It's not your fault," Abel sighed, rubbing his tired eyes. He glanced over at Harley who was still staring at the wall contemplatively. The dim light cast shadows across her face and around her eyes, making her expression look more severe than it was. She seemed to feel his stare and glanced over, making Abel blush and look away again.

"Anyway," he continued, "it doesn't matter now. I know and there's no changing that."

Harley opened her mouth and then shut it again. Deciding to go ahead and speak, she said, "You wanna see something cool?"

Confused, Abel nodded.

Harley stood up and grabbed Abel's HoloNet off of his desk. Sitting down in front of Abel this time, she hunched over slightly and began swiping on the Net. Finally, she handed it to Abel.

A blank, white screen stared back at Abel, light glaring brightly into his weary eyes and making him squint. "What am I looking for?" Abel asked.

A grin spread across Harley's face. "Your mom had disabled a lot of the Net's features to keep you from finding out too much. This particular feature is the database. It holds every piece of information that's public property...and some that aren't if you know how to find them."

"Okay...but what does it do?"

Her grin widened. "Now that's the cool part. It does whatever you want it to do with the right bit of coding. Right now since you're fairly new to all this, let's stick to basics: searching. You can find any information you want on here just by either using the voice activation and saying it or finding the right code, also known as searching."

"How do you use the voice activation?"

"Tap anywhere on the screen or you could do hands-free by using the activation word which is normally: 'Femater'. You can change it through programming, but that's usually the basic one," Harley explained.

Abel tapped the center of the screen and a beep issued forth from the glass-like, rectangular plate. "Males," Abel stated clearly.

Another beep sounded and instantaneously the white screen filled with different articles with the keyword 'male'. A robotic voice filled the room, saying, "Male: defined as an unethical, violent neanderthal incapable of complex thought. Males were eradicated over three hundred years ago due to their lack of civilization and sociopathic tendencies that often led to violence, chaos, and insubordination."

After the voice had stopped a holograph popped up of what Abel supposed was what they pictured as a male. A large, hairy monster-like creature covered in blood with exaggeratedly sharp teeth stared back at Abel. That circled around a few times before being replaced by a holo video of a male ('raised in captivity to be studied for scientific purposes', read the caption) that was being dissected.

"Turn it off! Turn it off!" Abel shouted.

Harley grabbed the HoloNet away from him and swiped and tapped a few times before the HoloVid disappeared. Feeling slightly nauseous, Abel glared at his bedsheets. This was what the world thought of him?

"Abel, I'm sorry. This wasn't supposed to—you weren't—I was just trying to show you—"

"Harley, it's fine. I have to learn this somewhere, don't I? It's not like my mom's going to tell me about it," he bitterly muttered.

Harley's head shot up. "Abel, I'm sure your mom had good reasons for doing what she did."

"You're taking her side?" he exclaimed.

"No. I'm not taking anyone's side. I just don't want you to hate your mother and especially not because of me. You have every right to be angry with her and I know this is all a huge shock, but try to see her side too, please."

Abel sighed, still feeling slightly betrayed. "Whatever," he exhaled.

Instantly he regretted it, though, as Harley's eyes filled with sadness and her face dropped. She tried to cover it up with an unconvincing smile, but Abel saw through it.

"I'm sorry. I'm just tired and my brain is fried and I have so much to think about."

"I know," Harley whispered with a genuine smile this time. "So back to my question from yesterday," she said, changing the subject, "how are males different from females?"

"Well, males tend to be larger, stronger—"

"No, not physically. Everyone is built differently, and that doesn't really matter. All women have different breasts." Abel's cheeks instantly glowed alive; he was pretty sure Harley could feel the heat radiating off them from across the room where she was sitting with her legs propped up on the edge of his desk. "All women have different heights, eye colors, everything. I meant mentally. You're obviously a thinking, breathing human with an equal intellect to me. You aren't a savage beast or an animal."

Abel shrugged. "I know as little as you on this. The only person I've ever interacted with is my mother."

Harley furrowed her eyebrows in thought. "Well, I guess we'll just have to find out together. It's getting late; I should probably leave. But I'll be back tomorrow."

"What about your school?"

Harley laughed. "As if I actually learn anything! All they do is push government propaganda. It used to be schooling, math, history, English, but as soon as you're promoted it switches. Men this, men that, evil, evil, evil. I swear, for a society that hates men so much, they sure seem to talk about them a lot. Anyway, I gotta go."

Abel tilted his head and bit his lip, letting out a small sigh. He didn't really want her to leave, but she definitely couldn't stay any longer. "Bye, Harley."

Harley smiled and waved. "See you tomorrow."

She left Abel's small room and as she was closing the door, Abel whispered to himself, "Thank you for saving me."

CHAPTER 8

His mother came down directly after she got home from work. Abel knew this confrontation was coming. There was no avoiding it.

She began talking as soon as Abel connected eyes with her. "I've given you time to cool off and to think, but I really must know: how did you find out about the extinction?"

The bomb dropped. Luckily, Abel had foreseen this."I discovered a block on my HoloNet and was curious to see why it was blocked, so I managed to unblock it and your coding unraveled, revealing all the lies you've been hiding from me."

Sarah sighed. "Accuse me all you want, but I did this for you."

Abel's anger flared up again at her words. "For me? When have you actually done anything for me? Do you even love me? Or am I just some burden to you?"

And just like that Abel triggered something in his mother that he had never seen before. Tears began welling up in her eyes and streaming done her cheeks and her lip trembled. "Don't you dare, Abel Christopher Williams. Don't ever say that again! If I didn't love you, if you were just a burden to me I would have let you die! I wouldn't have gone through all of the trouble to raise you in secret, to protect you. You don't even know the half of what I've been through for you, so don't you dare say that I don't love you!"

Before Abel could react, she slammed out of his room, but not before a loud sob escaped her lips.

Guilt flooded Abel's stomach, mixing with anger and confusion. Despite everything of course, he still loved his mother. And he felt terrible that he had caused her such pain, but at the same time he had been caused pain.

Not knowing what else to do, Abel decided he needed a nap. Flopping onto his bed, his heavy eyes almost instantly fell shut and he drifted off into a restless sleep.

CHAPTER 9

Abel didn't wake up until after his mother had already left (which he was grateful for because he wasn't sure he was ready to face her yet), but he did find his breakfast waiting for him at his desk. He ate it slowly and by the time he had finished, he could hear Harley upstairs.

As soon as she entered Abel's room, she began talking. "So I've been thinking.... You said your mother gave you a HSD, right?" Abel nodded. "Well, the purpose of them is to disguise a room as something else, right?" Abel nodded again confusedly. "Well, what if they could disguise something else?"

Abel frowned. "Like what?"

"You, dummy!"

Abel's eyes widened in comprehension. "You mean..."

Harley smiled. "Yup, let's try it!"

Harley darted over to Abel's desk and grabbed the small cube. "Okay, now all I have to do is reprogram the settings to your dimensions, add new graphics to the database, and...voila! Try it!" she said, shoving the device towards Abel.

Abel pressed a button on it and shoved the cube in his pocket. "So? Did it work?"

Harley grinned at Abel. "It did. You look like a girl! Wait...."

Abel felt his stomach drop with dread. "What?"

"Well, when you move too quickly, it sort of glitches."

Abel went to check his reflection in the mirror. His normally messy, black hair looked like loose curls that went down to his shoulders. His frame was more petite and he looked about seven inches shorter. His green eyes were larger and more delicate looking and instead of jeans and a t-shirt, he was wearing a knee-length dress. He definitely looked more girly. But then he jerked his hand up and down to check Harley's statement and he scrunched his nose in disapproval.

It wasn't anything too bad. Just the slightest glitch in the smoothness of the movement, making it momentarily look like he had two hands. But he had been moving his hand as quickly as possible to test the glitch and it was just a tiny, second-long flash.

"It's not too bad," Abel mused.

Harley shook her head. "No, not really. I think you'd be fine outside."

"It worked," he whispered to himself. "It worked!" he exclaimed to Harley.

Harley was laughing at his child-like enthusiasm. "If you liked your little stroll the other day, you're going to love what I have planned for today."

"Well, it wasn't exactly a stroll," Abel corrected.

She rolled her eyes. "Close enough."

Abel furrowed his brow in confusion, but Harley seemed to have moved on already. She was walking towards the stairs when she turned around to face him again.

She gave an impish grin and wiggled her eyebrows. Abel felt like jumping up and down. The excitement consumed him, making him forget the guilt and the dangers of leaving the house and his overwhelming confusion. "Let's go."

"Come on," Harley said, leading the way out of Abel's room and upstairs. "Are you hungry?" she asked as they walked down the street side by side.

"Sure," Abel said with a nod.

"That thing doesn't disguise your voice," Harley warned. "Be careful when you're talking in front of other people."

Abel nodded again and took in his surroundings. Harley had led him to a different street than his first time out. This one was much less colorful and more depressing. The sidewalk was cracked and the road was empty and strange. Overgrown bushes and trees hung low over the sidewalks and large roots escaped into the cracks and holes in the pavement. "Where are we?" Abel asked.

"Don't be deceived by the dreary exterior. Most people can't afford to live in the ritzy neighborhoods like you and me. This is a nice place though. I'm taking you to my favorite place to skip school. And the ladies here are a lot less likely to rat us out in case we get caught; they aren't too fond of the government."

"You skip school often?"

"It doesn't matter. No one notices anyway."

Abel frowned. "What do you mean 'no one notices'?"

"No one cares enough to notice."

Abel was silent. He wasn't quite sure how to respond to that, but for some reason he felt embarrassed. They walked on for a few more minutes until Harley pulled him inside a little diner on the side of the road. Abel was hit with the realization that he had never once dined anywhere but the confines of his room. It was an odd thought, that to anyone else would seem obvious or unimportant, but to Abel, this was his first *taste* of freedom.

"I know it doesn't look like much," Harley said with her smile slipping for the first time since Abel had met her, "but it's a pretty nice place. Just wait until you see the inside. It's pretty much the only place that still serves *good* bad-for-you food. Most of their recipes are over three hundred years old and they try to resource to actual farms instead of laboratories. It even has one of those tongue scanner things. They're kind of out of date, but I like them."

"Tongue scanner?"

Harley laughed at Abel's horrified expression. "It scans your tongue to find out what food you'd like best and then the kitchen prepares it for you."

Abel regarded the crumbling brick once more, feeling a sense of excitement wash over him.

"What if it glitches while I chew?" he wondered.

"We'll sit in the back and you can turn away from everyone else," Harley supplied. She always seemed to have the answers. "Come on."

As soon as they entered, calmness swept over Abel, despite the buzzing of activity. The brick carried throughout the restaurant, making up the flooring. A bar stood proudly gleaming at the front with white tiles and trays as far as the eye could see. Closest to

Abel was a platter of fudge, piled high to touch the top of the glass dome that had accumulated a thin layer of condensation.

Booths lined the walls and the center of the building, and despite the emptiness of the streets, nearly every table was full. Laughter, chatter, and soft music floated to Abel's ears and some mouthwatering smell filled his nostrils, dancing around his head and making him crave whatever it was. He stood in the doorway, taking it all in, but Harley, like always, seemed to be two steps ahead of him

"There s Cindy! She owns the place. Cindy!"

Cindy glanced over and did a double take. "Harley! And you've brought a friend! Who might you be, dear?"

Abel panicked. They hadn't thought of a fake name for him.

"This is Abbey," Harley introduced, not missing a beat.

Cindy held her hand out towards Abel and he stared at it for a moment. Harley began jerking her head violently towards Cindy's outstretched hand behind Cindy's back. Comprehension dawned on Abel and he took Cindy's hand, moving it up and down slightly. "It's nice to meet you, Abbey."

Abel smiled at the woman uncomfortably. Harley seemed to notice his strain and moved along towards a booth. Abel accidentally bonked into a grumpy looking woman and she turned to glare at him. She held up a fist with one finger pointing up and Abel tilted his head, moving along behind Harley who was holding back giggles.

When they had been seated, Abel leaned forward and whispered, "What was that all about?"

Harley laughed. "She flipped you off."

"She flipped what now?"

"It's a vulgar hand gesture used when you're angry or don't like someone. Don't go around doing that. That's just Marge. The government just evicted her and repossessed her children."

"They can do that?"

"They can do whatever they want."

Abel was getting more and more confused by this complex outside world. Maybe his basement *was* better. "Come on. Let's order," Harley suggested.

Abel shrugged and watched Harley as she grabbed a small device off of the table. She held it up to her face and opened her mouth widely. The device issued a high-pitched beep and Harley handed it to Abel. He stared at it for a moment before repeating what Harley had done. A long beep sounded and Abel set the scanner back on the table.

"The food will be out in a few minutes," Harley informed.

Abel nodded while looking around the small restaurant. He had never known out of date or in date or anything of the sort, so to him the whole diner was amazing. Harley had said it was retro, trying to replicate what a high-tech restaurant looked like BME. There was even a television in the corner! Abel had read about those.

Harley smiled at Abel. "Okay, *Abbey*. Here comes our food."

Abel turned his head slightly and saw a platter of food hovering towards them. The platter set itself down on the table and Harley gesticulated for him to take his plate. "What is it?" Abel asked.

"You've never seen a chili dog before?" Abel shook his head. "Well, they aren't very common anymore," Harley continued, "but Cindy likes things that are uncommon."

"And what about the drink?" Abel asked.

"A milkshake? You've never had one of those either?" Abel shook his head again. "You poor, poor deprived child. Your mother must be very cruel. Just try some."

Abel took a sip. It was a lot thicker than he had expected and a lot colder. "Ach!" he exclaimed, grabbing his throat with one hand.

Harley was guffawing so hard she was snorting. "Yeah, I should have warned you about that," she managed to get out between her laughs.

"What was that torture?" Abel asked.

"That, my friend, is brain-freeze."

"But it wasn't in my brain."

"Just try it again, but slower this time."

Abel looked hesitantly at his cup. He slowly took another sip. It was sweet and tasted like some sort of fruit and chocolate. Raspberries, maybe. Abel loved raspberries. "This is amazing," he marveled.

Harley was still laughing. "It's so cute how much you don't know."

Abel frowned. "Cute?"

"Don't tell me you've never heard of that before either. Adorable, charming, endearing?"

"I know what cute is," Abel snapped.

Harley just laughed despite Abel's harsh tone. Abel grumbled slightly and continued eating his chili dog and milkshake. When they had both finished Harley paid, handing over a small, glass-like card with blue flashing numbers and letters on the surface.

After having paid, Harley grabbed hold of Abel's arm and pulled him to whatever she had planned next.

They walked for a little while until they reached a building labeled ZOO. "I've read about these," Abel said. "Isn't it where they keep animals for viewing?"

"Sort of," Harley confirmed. "It's a little different now." She sounded almost wistful.

"How so?"

"You'll see."

Harley walked through the door and led Abel inside. Lining the walls, were glass panels and behind each panel, was a different animal. "Wow," Abel breathed. "I've seen pictures, but they aren't anything compared to this."

"Just wait," Harley said.

They approached the first glass panel, a penguin. It waddled up to the glass and stared at them. Harley touched the glass and a voice began spewing facts about penguins and inside the penguin's habitat, the penguin stiffened and began dancing.

"Penguins can dance?"

"Well, kind of," Harley explained. "The zoologists discovered a way to control the animal's body."

Abel's eyes widened. "What?! That's horrible. That's sick."

He stormed out of the building, not wanting to see anymore mind control of the poor animals. Abel felt like crying. How could anyone find that amusing?

"Abel, wait!" Harley cried, running to try to catch up with him. "Abel," she panted.

He whipped around. "How do you like that? How can you watch that? Do you know what it's like to not have any free will? Do you understand what it's like to have no freedom of choice?"

"Abel, calm down. I took you there for a reason. I *do* understand. I took you there to show you how cruel this world's become, what the government is capable of. Don't you understand the implications of this? If they can control those animals, you can sure bet they can control humans too. They say the world is so much better without men, but look at what they're doing. Abel, I can assure you that this part of our trip wasn't for your enjoyment."

Abel felt embarrassed all of a sudden. He looked at his feet and cleared his throat. "So if the government can literally control us, how do we know that we aren't being influenced by them right now?"

"They have to implant a device in your brain."

"Well, that's morbid," Abel mumbled.

Harley nodded with her mouth drawn in a grim line. "It is," she agreed.

Abel was growing more and more shocked with the outside world. It wasn't at all how he'd expected it to be, it wasn't at all how books portrayed it. His stomach ached slightly and he wasn't sure if it was from the food or what he had just seen. He felt incredibly overwhelmed.

"Can we call it quits for today?" Abel asked, pressing his eyes shut.

"Yeah, sure. I know it's a lot to absorb."

Harley helped him home and walked him to the basement. Instantly after she had left, Abel collapsed on his bed and fell asleep, tired from the long day.

CHAPTER 10

Harley was there again, bright and early after Sarah had left. Abel was ready to explore more. After having all night to soak in all he had seen and learned the day before, he ached to go outside again.

They walked down the same empty, cracked street they had yesterday, passing the crumbling diner and continuing to the end of the road before making a left.

"Where are we going?" Abel asked while glancing around the even more overgrown scenery.

"I'll give you a few hints, but that's it," Harley said with a smirk. "It's very wet. It involves aerobic exercise. And it's fun."

To anyone else this may have been a dead giveaway, but it left Abel even more confused than before.

Abel nodded, deciding not to press the point, and followed behind Harley for a little longer until she stopped at another building. "This is a waterpark," she told Abel.

"Waterpark? As in a place where you go to play in liquid?"

Harley nodded. "The very same."

She led the way through the abandoned building to the main office. There was a booth that Harley approached and pressed a few buttons. "Two," she said in an even voice, sticking the same glass-like card into a slot until a dinging sound was emitted.

The machine clicked and whirred and finally said in a monotonous, robotic voice, "Have a good time and remember: safety is the best fun there is! Please stay and listen to the rules before entering the park! Rule one: never...."

"Come on," Harley ushered, ignoring the machine's instructions and walking through the gate.

Abel followed Harley out the backdoor and towards what he assumed was the water. When they got outside, Abel halted in his tracks to marvel at the sight in front of him. About thirty bubbles of water balanced in midair with a giant pool on the ground beneath them. The water bubbles swayed slightly, moving back and forth about an inch or two.

"This is incredible," Able whispered.

Harley giggled. "This is one of my favorite things to do when I skip."

"Do you think the HSD will work if it's wet?" Abel asked.

"It's pretty high-tech stuff, Abel. You could live at the bottom of ocean and that thing would still work."

Abel didn't respond because he was too busy staring at the water. Harley began climbing one of the ladder-like things on the side of the ground pool. When she got to the top, she plunged into the highest floating pool fully clothed and dove to the bottom. She flipped out of that bubble and into one beneath her, repeating this until she was in the ground pool. Abel sat at the side and dipped his feet in. He didn't know how to swim. It wasn't really something you needed to know when you stayed in the same room every day of your life.

Harley swam up to where he was sitting and grabbed his ankle, pulling him in. Abel spluttered and flailed his arms wildly as Harley busted up laughing. Abel realized that the water was only about four feet deep where he was and blushed.

"I knew that," he grumbled.

Once Harley had composed herself, she told him to lie on his stomach. "Just float for a few seconds."

Abel did as he was told and waited for further instructions. "Okay, now kick your legs."

He began to violently thrash his legs around, splashing water everywhere and moving him nowhere. Harley shook her head and said, "No, less erratically. Up and down."

Abel frowned and tried again. Still not moving anywhere, Abel blushed and stopped.

"Like this," Harley instructed, gliding easily to behind Abel. She grabbed his ankles and gently moved them up and down separately.

Abel jerked himself away. "I don't like being touched."

"Sorry," Harley apologized awkwardly. "Uh, try again."

Abel tried to smooth the awkward tension by flipping back onto his stomach and trying the way Harley had shown him. "Good!" Harley praised. "Put your arms out. No, straight. There you go! Keep your legs out."

Soon Abel was unskillfully lapping around the pool.

Harley glanced at the sky. "We'd better go. It's getting late again."

Abel agreed and they made their way home without talking. He was content, happy even. And Harley seemed equally at ease. Maybe the outside wasn't so bad.

CHAPTER 11

The weekend was torturous for Abel. No Harley, no waterparks, no adventures, no new. Just his four walls, time-passers, and the occasional visit from his mother that normally went something like this:

Sarah: "Hi, sweetheart."

Abel: Grunts.

Sarah: "I brought you dinner."

Abel: Grunts again.

Whenever she came down, it made Abel feel guilty and stressed, not to mention the unresolved conflict. The tension was so palpable that Sarah got to the point where she only came down at mealtimes. He was surprised she hadn't caught on to him by now; he was being fairly obvious. But still, Abel thought of only the outside world: the good and the bad.

When Monday finally rolled around, Abel paced his room, waiting for the sound of his mother leaving. He heard the front door open and close and waited impatiently for the sound of Harley fumbling downstairs.

"Hey," she smiled upon entering his room. "How does a day in sound? I thought I could teach you a little more about the Nets and coding and stuff."

"Cool," Abel grinned.

He pulled over his HoloNet and turned it on, revealing the news. Top headlines flashed red: Hacker Red Dragon Strikes Again.

"Who's the Red Dragon?" Abel asked Harley.

"They're a hacker that attacks government files and computers. The government--especially Chancellor Mia--hates them because whoever it is makes them look incompetent."

Intrigued, Abel tapped the article and began reading aloud. "The Red Dragon, cyber hacker and felon, strikes again in the Department of Public Safety and Criminal Prevention."

"That's Hillary's department," Harley gasped.

"Officials say that it is still unclear the purpose of these attacks and the files that have been stolen or altered. 'We are doing everything we can to ensure your security and to retrieve the files that have been affected,' says department official," Abel continued.

"Wow," Harley laughed, "they don't even know what the Red Dragon did."

"Who is the Red Dragon?" Abel asked.

"No one knows," Harley said with a shrug. "She never reveals her true identity and she's never been caught. She's like an apparition."

Abel continued to stare at the Net for a little while longer before glancing back up at Harley. "So what are we learning today?"

She grinned and took the HoloNet from Abel. "Minor coding. You'll be surprised by what you can with just some minor coding knowledge."

And so they dove in, Harley showing him about codes and manipulating them to do exactly what you wanted. By the end of the day, Abel could find the cheats for a game and use them accordingly.

Abel laughed at himself. "Wow, that's useful. I'm so good at coding."

Harley smiled. "Everyone starts somewhere."

CHAPTER 12

The next day Abel was up bright and early, waiting for Harley. His mother left his breakfast like usual and then departed for work.

Soon, Harley poked her head into Abel's room and smiled.

"You ready, dork?" Abel grabbed the HSD and turned it on, putting it in his pocket. "Very feminine. Let's go."

Abel followed a few feet behind Harley as she led outside. "Where to today?"

"Today we're doing something special. And very important, so don't mess this up."

Abel felt nervous. "No pressure," he muttered.

It was like the first time he'd seen Harley: his hands were shaking and his palms were sweating.

"Come on, Abe. It'll be fine; *you'll* be fine."

"My name isn't Abe."

"I know. It's a nickname."

"Nickname?"

"You know...a nickname. Something you call someone other than their name. Usually a shortened version of it; Abe for Abel or maybe Har for Harley."

"But why? Why not just address them by their proper name?"

"Well, usually, a nickname is a term of endearment...or maybe the opposite depending on the person."

"Which one is it?"

"What?" Harley asked.

"Which one is it this time: a term of endearment or the opposite?" Abel clarified with his eyes glued to the ground.

"What do you think, idiot?"

"I don't know. You insult me a lot. Dummy, dork, idiot...."

Harley laughed. "Did you actually get offended by those?"

Abel blushed and kept his eyes on the ground.

Harley stopped walking and faced Abel. "Look, those insults...aren't insults. They're me joking around. You're my friend, okay? Sometimes I just forget how little you understand about social cues."

Abel nodded and Harley began walking again. Abel trailed behind her and she turned off the road. "Uh, Harley? Where are you going?"

"I can't tell you right now. We might be overheard."

"Overheard?"

"Just stop talking for a few minutes, okay?"

"But—"

"Abel," Harley scolded. She sounded dead serious and Harley was rarely serious. Abel listened.

She tiptoed through the forest carefully and Abel followed behind her, trying not to trip on exposed roots or slip on dead leaves.

Harley stopped abruptly and held out her arm to stop Abel too. "I think this is it..." she whispered to herself.

She prodded around on a tree next to her and eventually pulled on a branch that opened a staircase on the forest floor next Harley's feet. "Come on," she whispered, walking down the steps. "Close it behind yourself," she instructed Abel.

He followed her down and closed the hatch, encasing them in total darkness. Abel was pretty used to the dark and his eyes adjusted quickly, but Harley stayed glued to where she was for a solid seven minutes. Abel waited slightly impatiently due to his increasing curiosity.

Finally, Harley began moving again. They descended three flights of stairs when it evened out into a long hallway. It was about ninety yards long and at the end there was an old wooden door. Harley opened the door to reveal a round room filled with chairs and a stage at the center. There were about two-hundred women contained in the room, chatting quietly amongst themselves.

"What are we doing here?" Abel finally asked.

"You'll see," was Harley's only answer.

A woman mounted the stage and everyone instantly fell silent. "Thank you all for joining us today," the woman said. "Today our meeting is concerning the rumors about the government...doing away with the elderly. Our sources say that Femater is planning on enacting a law that no one over the age of sixty will be allowed to live due to their lack of productivity. They are going to disguise this law as a retirement plan.

"Overpopulation. They attribute this to the high success rate of curing illnesses. And they also have found a way to blame men, I'm sure. Would anyone like to speak to this?"

Harley stood. "I would like to speak to it, Chancellor Keturah Beauregard"

"Keturah?" Abel whispered to Harley.

During his time away from Harley, Abel had been doing as much research as possible to get him up to date on everything. Keturah was leader of Masculum which was an organization for male rights.

"I have brought proof that men are not as they are portrayed by Femater," Harley continued, ignoring Abel.

"What proof have you?" asked Keturah.

"Abel, take off the HSD," Harley whispered to him.

"What? No! Are you trying to get me killed?"

"Do you trust me?"

"What—"

"Do...you... *trust*...me?"

"I-I.... Yes, I trust you," Abel decided.

"Take off the HSD," Harley repeated.

Abel uncertainly removed the device from his pocket and turned it off. The crowd gave a collective gasp and Keturah's mouth hung agape. "How— What—"

"This is Abel," Harley shouted over the murmurs. "He is an eighteen-year-old *male*."

"Abel?" a woman with caramel-colored hair asked, standing up.

Abel's mind reeled at the sight of the all-too-familiar woman that had said his name.

CHAPTER 13

Sarah Williams was standing among this group of Masculumians and she did not look happy. "Mom?" Abel gasped.

"Abel Christopher Williams, you'd better explain yourself this instant! Do you realize the danger you're in?"

"Mom, what are you doing here?"

"I could ask you the same thing, Abel. I happen to be here for you, fighting for male rights. What are *you* doing here?"

"Fighting for male rights. I, um, kind of snuck out a few days ago and bumped into Harley. She's been helping me ever since."

"Harley? Harley Haim?"

"In the flesh," Harley responded.

"Hillary's sister?"

Harley tensed up at the mention of her sister's name. Abel ached for how defensive—that was the word for it, right? —she had become. It must have been a prison to be her sister, somehow. Harley had heard all of the stories about her sister, witty wonderful anecdotes, how pretty she was... and he hoped my mom wouldn't join in the crowd. Abel wasn't sure he'd be able to stand by and let his mother do that.

"God, I hate that! It's always Hillary this and Hillary that. I'm a person too, you know!"

"I was just going to say that I'm glad you're nothing like your sister. And thank you for taking care of my son."

Harley looked shocked, but quickly recovered. "You're welcome."

The murmurs of the women surrounding them had crescendoed so that it was unbearably loud. Abel felt himself becoming overwhelmed.

Abel's hands felt clammy as everyone stared at him, pointing and whispering.

"Go on, Abel," Harley prompted.

"Uh, I'm, uh, Abel. A guy...obviously." But he was unheard over all the talking. He felt even more nervous. He cleared his throat and started again.

"I'm Abel and—"

"*HEY!*" Harley yelled, grabbing the attention of everyone in the room and silencing the conversations. "I know you have questions and I know you're surprised, but show him some respect. He's trying to explain."

"I'm Abel," he said for the third time, "and I'm a male. And I, uh, don't want to kill anyone...." There were a few snickers throughout the room. "I'm actually not violent at all."

"How is this possible?" a woman in the back shouted.

"Why haven't you presented yourself to us before now?"

"What are men actually like?"

The questions kept pouring out and overwhelming Abel's brain. He thought he might explode if he was asked one more thing.

"Please, everyone," Harley exclaimed, "let him tell his story and then ask your questions one at a time. This is all new to him and we don't want to overstimulate him."

"Tell us, Abel," Keturah prompted, "everything."

And so for the second time, Abel told his story. It came more quickly this time, more readily. At first he was nervous, but the more he talked the less timid he was and the more he was articulate. Once he had finished his story, there was silence and Abel began to feel anxious again. He wiped his hands on his jeans.

Then, a woman stood and began clapping and soon the entire audience was erupting in applause. And then a woman at the very front of the crowd touched Abel's chest. Abel was just about to jerk away when another hand touched him on his back. And then another and another. All the women were trying to touch him. But seeing as there wasn't enough room, the women ended up just touching each other--shoulders, arms--making a giant web, connection everyone in the room.

And Abel hated it. It was beautiful and symbolic, but he hated being touched by so many different people and the moment it was over he felt like he could finally breathe again.

Keturah stood again and cleared her throat. "As you can see, males are not our issue; we are males' issue! This is what our revolution is all about. We can do this; we can show them how wrong they are. Abel is just the kind of proof we needed in this pivotal time. Remember: every voice counts. We meet every Monday. Meeting adjourned."

Harley nudged Abel with a grin. "See," she bragged, "I was right."

"My mom...."

And surely enough, Sarah was marching over to where Harley and Abel were standing....

CHAPTER 14

"Abel, why did you leave the house?! Do you understand the danger this puts you in?"

Abel winced at his mom's harsh tone. "I understand the danger, Mom! You remind me every day. But Harley was in danger too!"

"Safety was supposed to be your number one priority! This," she gestured wildly around the room, "is not safe!"

"But Harley figured out a way to disguise me! Everyone thinks I'm a girl when I leave the house."

"I don't care! What if that thing malfunctioned? What if it broke? What if—"

"What if, what if, what if? If we spent our whole lives thinking about the 'what ifs', we'd never do anything!"

"I'm here fighting for your rights. I'm here changing things for you."

"I understand that now! But you never told me that before! To me it was: I'm going to live in this room until I die," Abel exclaimed.

Sarah seemed at a loss for words. "Your safety is top priority. You're going back home and you will not step foot out of your room. No time-passers for two months. March, mister." She pointed towards the door and Abel turned the HSD back on, trudging out towards the hallway. "It was nice meeting you, Harley."

Harley didn't say anything and that made Abel panic. Had his mom scared her off? Was this the last time he'd ever see her?

Abel turned back to look at her, trying to save her face in his mind. Harley winked at him and Abel couldn't stop the grin that slowly spread across his face. She'd find a way to break him out again; Abel just knew it. So he complied with his mother, letting her lead him out of the dark, underground room, into the hallway, and up the secret staircase that let out at the heavily foliaged forest floor. They got back to their house without trouble and Abel returned to his room.

His mother walked in behind him and closed the door. "I'm installing a new security system to ensure you do not leave your room. You are the future, Abel. We can't take any risks."

Abel didn't argue and Sarah left. Abel sat on his bed and closed his eyes. Harley's face popped into his head and Abel smiled. Friend, his brain recognized. It felt good to have a friend. Thinking of Harley made him feel all warm and fuzzy inside. His thoughts shifted to the meeting.

He didn't know there were any revolutionists, let alone his mother. Abel curled up into a ball and tucked himself under the covers. He might as well sleep seeing as Harley wouldn't be coming back until tomorrow.

He could faintly hear his mother puttering around upstairs, probably installing some new security system. Abel smiled to himself, knowing that Harley would probably be able to hack whatever his mother had bought.

When Abel finally drifted off to sleep, his thoughts were still on Harley, leaving his mind fuzzy with images of her hair blowing wildly in the wind, casting the smell of coconuts everywhere. Images of her crystal blue eyes, piercing his soul.

CHAPTER 15

The next morning when Sarah went down to give Abel breakfast, she expressly warned him to not leave the house and informed him that the security systems had been installed. Abel just smiled and nodded to everything she said, knowing that Harley was most likely waiting outside for Abel's mother to leave the house.

As soon as Abel's mom departed for work, noises could be heard from the stairway. Abel grabbed the HSD that his mother had forgotten to confiscate and turned it on.

"I see you're ready to go," Harley said from behind him. "You know you're my favorite girlfriend, right?"

Abel jumped slightly because he hadn't heard her enter, but smiled and faced her. "Let's go."

"Come on then, Abbey."

Abel followed Harley out of the house as she led the way down the street. She was telling him something about weather, but Abel couldn't focus on the words she was saying. He was too enamored with thoughts of what they were going to do.

"So where are we going?" Abel asked.

"Today we are going to a sporting event."

"Like soccer?"

"Kind of," Harley conceded. "Today we're going to watch one of the only sports that's still continued: basketball. The rest have sort of died out because there really isn't anyone to play and there *really* isn't anyone to watch."

"Basketball? Like the round ball through the hoop? Sounds kind of juvenile if you ask me."

Harley laughed at Abel's statement. "It's a little more complicated than that."

"What could possibly make it difficult?" Abel queried.

"Hand-eye coordination," Harley said with a shrug. "Clumsiness, lack of skills needed to play the sport, the defense."

Abel nodded though he had never really understood the point of basketball.

They arrived and a large court surrounded by bleachers. Harley paid for entry and the two found seats towards the center; most of the seats were empty as it was. The games started soon after and Abel had a difficult time following, but he enjoyed it nonetheless.

About halfway through, Harley got up to get Abel and herself snacks. Abel was slightly nervous about being alone in such a crowded area, but he didn't say anything. While Harley was gone, whenever someone looked at Abel, his heart leapt into his throat.

Harley returned after a few minutes and handed Abel and pink, cloud-like thing on a stick and a bottle of water. Able stared at the fluffy, pink thing until Harley glanced over and began laughing. "It's cotton candy."

"Cotton? Like the material used to make clothes?" Abel only knew this because his mother had to hand make clothes for him; who would sell male clothes now that there were no males?

"It's food," Harley assured. "Try some."

Abel hesitated, but then remembered how Harley had never steered him wrong. He took a large bite and was shocked by the sweet, sugary flavor. But then it began to melt away. "It just disappeared!" Abel cried in surprise.

"Yeah, it dissolves," Harley explained.

Needless to say, the cotton candy was gone very quickly.

When the game ended, it still only noonish, so Harley led Abel down the road a little more. Something hit Abel on the shoulder and he jumped. "What was that?" he exclaimed.

"What?" Harley asked with a quizzical expression.

Abel reached up and felt where it had hit; a cold, wet spot was on his shirt. "That," Able said, motioning to his shirt.

Harley held her hand palm up and stood still for a little while. "It's raining!"

Little dots littered the pavement and water began to fall from the sky frivolously. "What's going on?"

"It's raining," Harley repeated.

"Rain?"

"You know...rain. When water evaporates into the air and forms clouds, the water eventually has to be released."

"The sky is crying," Abel summed up, only half joking.

"Sure, Abel. The sky is crying."

Light flashed through the air and it was followed by a loud *BOOM!* Abel jumped and fell flat to the ground.

"Uh, Abel...what are you doing?"

"There was gunfire!"

"That was lightning and thunder, idiot." "Lightning is the release of zinc into the atmosphere. Lightning does not make noise."

"Sure it does," Harley argued. "Lightning is a very concentrated form of electricity. When it hits the ground, it creates the sound of an explosion."

Abel got into a sitting position. "So you're telling me that lightning is a giant bolt of electricity that hits the ground at a high enough velocity to create ground-shaking noise in order to calm me down."

"The odds of getting struck by lightning are, like, one in seven-hundred thousand."

"I like those odds," Abel granted, standing up.

Another bolt flashed across the sky, followed by a deafening boom. Abel jumped again. Harley was trying not to laugh as she continued walking. "It's not funny," Abel whined.

Harley just shook her head. "Let's just go home since it's pouring and we're soaked."

Harley and Abel walked briskly back to Abel's house, shivering and Abel jumping every so often after a clap of thunder. Abel was turning around to say goodbye to Harley when the rain slowly let up and the clouds cleared. Harley smiled and pointed at a colorful semicircle in the sky.

"What is it?" Abel inquired.

"It's a rainbow," Harley explained, "a colorful arc formed in the sky by reflection, refraction, and dispersion of light in water droplets resulting in a spectrum of light appearing in the sky."

Abel stared at it for a few minutes before saying, completely joking, "The sky is smiling now."

CHAPTER 16

That night when his mom came down to give him supper, Abel grabbed her arm to stop her from returning back upstairs. "Mom? I'm sorry. I never meant to hurt your feelings, but I was so confused at the time and all this new information had been dumped on me and I was angry. But I understand now. You had your reasons for doing what you did."

Sarah smiled at him warmly, wrapping her arms around him. "I'm sorry too. I know you were going through a lot. I love you, Abel."

"I love you too," he responded, not hesitating to return her hug.

They talked for a little while longer until Sarah decided to head up to bed.

Abel's mind was much too awake to sleep, so instead he pulled out his HoloNet and practiced his coding for a little bit. He still wasn't very good. He was about to shut off his Net when he decided to check the news holos one more time.

Again glaring in big red letters was a headline about the Red Dragon.

Abel didn't know why the Red Dragon intrigued him so much, but she did. He wondered if she went to the Masculum meetings. She was obviously rebelling against Chancellor Mia, but why? Knowing none of his questions had answers, Abel turned off the HoloNet and went to sleep.

When Abel woke up, Harley was sitting at his desk and rifling through some holos and papers. Abel wasn't quite sure how to react. He was certainly surprised to see her there and confused as to why she was there so early.

"What time is it?" Abel asked.

Harley glanced at Abel. "It's past ten."

Abel rubbed his eyes and rolled out of bed. "Why didn't you wake me up?"

Harley looked down at her lap. Was she embarrassed? That didn't compute in Abel's brain; Harley was always so unabashed about everything. "You looked so peaceful; I didn't want to disturb you," Harley said.

Abel grabbed the HoloSim device, but Harley took his wrist and stopped him. "You won't need that today."

"Why not?"

"We aren't going out," Harley explained.

Abel was confused. "What?"

"We are staying in today."

"Okay...?"

"Besides," Harley pointed out, "you're still in your jammies."

Abel looked down as though this thought hadn't occurred to him. Sure enough, he was wearing a pair of flannel pajama pants and an old t-shirt. He shrugged. Harley stood and walked out of Abel's room. "Where are you going if we aren't leaving?"

"Oh, we're leaving your room. We just aren't leaving the house."

Abel shrugged again and followed Harley upstairs. She had closed all of the curtains and dimmed the lights. "So what now?" asked Abel.

"Does your mom have any board games?" questioned Harley.

"Sure. On weekends she would come down and play with me. She told me that they were her great, great, great grandmother's. Apparently they don't make board games anymore, but since they don't make any noise, Mom loved to use them as a time-passer."

"Do you know where she keeps them?"

"Your guess is as good as mine," Abel mumbled. "Why the interest in board games?"

"I read a HoloBook where the characters played one and it sounds like fun. Low tech, but fun."

"Well, let's start looking, but remember: leave no evidence that you were ever there."

They scoured the house in search of the board games. In the end, it was Harley who found them (isn't it always). Abel was slightly angry and he couldn't put his finger on why. Maybe it was because he couldn't even find a board game in *his own house.* Harley seemed to notice his change of mood, but she didn't comment.

"So which one do you want to play first?"

"Something easy since you've never even seen a board game before."

"Oh ho! Are you saying that I'm not capable of playing a difficult game?"

"What? No, that isn't—I wasn't—uh, you are—"

"Joking, Abe; I'm joking."

Abel was embarrassed that he'd taken her seriously. He focused on the cabinet in front of him. Harley was laughing and soon Abel was laughing too. When they had both sobered up, Harley instructed Abel to pick the hardest game they had.

He contemplated his choices before pulling out Trivia Pursuit: BME. It was so hard because it asked random trivia about BME, a time period which neither Harley nor Abel knew much about. Abel explained the rules to Harley, and on the second round she won.

They were about to set up a different game when there was a loud pounding on the door. Harley gasped. "Be quiet," she whispered urgently. "Stay low and follow me."

Harley quickly rushed Abel downstairs. "What about the board games?" asked Abel. They hadn't had time to clean them up.

"I'll take care of it. Whatever you do, don't leave this room," Harley said, shutting Abel's door before he could argue.

Abel was as silent as possible, listening to all the noises above. He could hear Harley rushing to pack away the board games. The pounding on the front door sounded again. Abel's heart pounded with it and blood rushed in his ears.

Abel heard voices. Harley's voice...and someone else. Abel strained his ears to hear their conversation.

"What are you doing in Sarah Williams's house? Did you break in?"

"What does it matter, Hillary?"

Hillary? Harley's sister? How did she know Harley was here?

"It matters because this is a federal crime! This is a government official's house! I can't sweep everything under the rug for you!"

"Then don't, Hillary! I don't care. Wouldn't want to risk your perfect reputation, would you, though? This isn't about me and you know it."

"Harley, you make it sound like I don't care about you—"

"You don't! You just want that stupid promotion to Senior Administrator of the Department of Public Safety and Criminal Prevention."

"Harley—"

"Why are you even here? How'd you find me?"

"Your teacher told me that you've missed an excessive amount of school in the past month. She said you were absent again today which I thought was weird because you definitely left for school."

"How did you find me?" Harley repeated.

"I tracked your HoloCom."

Harley swore.

"Listen, Harley, I don't know what you were doing here or why you broke in, but if you leave now with me, I won't tell anyone you were here and I won't involve the government."

Harley was silent for a few seconds before saying. "Fine. I'll go with you. It's not like I was doing anything important anyway." She raised her voice slightly. "I won't come back today."

"Only today?" Hillary asked.

"Well, I can't exactly come back now that you've caught me," Harley conceded. She raised her voice again. "Too bad, too. I was going to come back tomorrow."

Abel smiled. She was sending him a message.

"Come on, Harley. And if I catch you here again, I will report you."

Abel heard the front door close and he shook his head. Harley sure was something. Abel knew she'd be back tomorrow and he knew she'd find a way to fix it so that no one could find her. Because that was Harley. Harley was the kind of girl that would do anything for what she believes in and for those she cares about. Abel liked being cared about.

CHAPTER 17

Harley came back the next day, just as she had hinted she would. Abel asked how she had managed to avoid a situation like yesterday.

"I planted my HoloCom at school, so if Hillary checks, it'll look like I'm there. I hacked into the school's files and changed it so that I was officially unenrolled, that way I won't show up on attendance."

"So what's the agenda today?"

"We are going to my house."

"Your house?"

"My house," Harley confirmed.

"Why?"

"Always questions, questions, questions. Can't you just roll with it?"

Abel gave Harley a flat look. "I don't roll."

"Course you don't, big guy."

"Are you mocking me?"

"He can be taught, people!"

Abel furrowed his eyebrows. Harley chuckled and handed Abel the Holographic Simulation Device. She led down the street a little ways before stopping. Harley hadn't been lying when she had said that she lived nearby. Her house was right around the corner from Abel's.

Abel followed her inside. "Hillary should have already left for work," Harley said. "I just have to grab a few things and then we can go."

Harley turned down a hall and disappeared into a room. She was gone for under five minutes when she returned again. "Okay, let's go," Harley said.

Abel walked out the front door and turned to talk to Harley, but she wasn't beside him. He turned around and Harley came rushing out the door. "Sorry," she apologized. "I had to delete the security footage. I have to do it every time we leave your house too."

"So what are we doing today?" asked Abel.

"I want to show you something."

Abel didn't ask what she wanted to show him because he figured that she would get annoyed. All Abel ever did was ask questions.

Harley detoured from the road and down a little forest trail that was almost impossible to see. Abel followed closely behind her so he didn't get lost; Harley twisted and turned and changed directions until they came upon a clearing overlooking untouched forest followed by a mountain range.

"Where are we?" asked Abel.

Harley gave Abel a sad smile. "This is my favorite place. It's untouched by people, government, propaganda, lies, wars, revolutions. It's peaceful."

"It's beautiful," Abel breathed. "It's...it's amazing. I've never seen anything like this before.... Duh, that probably sounded really stupid."

Harley laughed.

Abel glanced over at her. The wind was blowing her hair all over the place and her eyes were shut serenely. "Can I ask you a question?" Abel asked.

Harley raised an eyebrow with her eyes still closed. "You just did."

Abel shook his head despite the fact that she couldn't see it. "How are you so good at all this coding and stuff?"

Harley popped one eye open. "Can you keep a secret?"

Abel gave her a flat look and she laughed, "Oh, come on!"

Abel shook his head.

Harley sighed "Okay, fine. Being serious now. But you really can't tell anyone."

He nodded, eagerly waiting for her response.

She sucked in a deep breath and blurted out in a rush, "I'm the Red Dragon."

"Stop joking around," he said, shoving her arm.

"I'm serious! I'm the one hacking into the government and stuff. I started out doing it independently, but Keturah caught me one time; I was so sure that I was going to jail, but she helped me and introduced me to the revolution."

"You're-you're the Red Dragon?"

"In the flesh," Harley said with a soft smile.

"No way! Why didn't you tell me before?"

Harley shrugged. "I don't know. I guess because I was more focused on you."

Abel blushed and closed his eyes, letting the soft breeze encompass him.

"That was actually really relieving to tell someone. Besides, we're even now; I know your secret and you know mine."

Harley looked over at Abel and a look of determination crossed her face. "Abel, we could...we could run away together. Leave this town behind, this society. We could survive by ourselves."

Abel seriously considered this and the choice he made was probably the hardest one he'd ever have to make. He wanted this so badly. He wanted to be free.

"No. I'm sorry. I can't tell you how much I want that, but I can't leave my mother and what about male rights? Who's going to fight for it if not me?"

Harley looked at her feet and nodded. "I understand. You're very noble, Abel. I'm not sure I'd be able to make the same choice if I were in your position."

"Sure you would. You're a good person and you care about others. You didn't kill me," Abel reminded.

Harley laughed. "Abel, you are so crazy."

Abel smiled. "Crazy for you."

"What? What is this? Did Abel Williams just make a joke?" Harley joked, placing her hand over her heart.

"I suppose I did," Abel agreed.

CHAPTER 18

Harley snuck Abel out every day until the weekend, doing random things like trying to teach him to play basketball (as it turns out, Harley was actually not that great at sports), bringing him to the waterpark, showing him music and how to play.

Abel went all weekend by himself with just his mother. She didn't seem to know about the sneak outs and if she did she didn't say anything. When Monday came around, Abel was shocked when his mother came down and told him that he would be going to the revolutionary meeting with her.

"Grab the HSD, Abel. You're coming with me."

"Really?" Abel said in excitement.

"Yes, come on."

"Can we, uh, stop to, uh, get Harley?"

Abel's mother sighed. "I suppose."

Abel cheered and Sarah shook her head with a laugh. "Let's go," Abel said, switching on the HSD.

Abel's mother led outside and Harley came bounding up to them as soon as they exited their house. She had obviously been waiting to sneak Abel out and was clearly shocked to see him and his mom walking outside together.

"Mrs. Williams," she greeted.

"Abel," she said in an undertone.

"Hey, Harley," Abel responded with an impish grin.

"We were just going to go shopping," Mrs. Williams said to Harley with a wink.

Harley seemed to understand the code because she said, "I'll help you."

Abel, Harley, and Mrs. Williams followed the same path as the first time, the same secret stairway and the same long hallway, letting out into the circular room. Abel's mom led to the back of the room and took a seat, Abel sat beside her, and Harley sat beside Abel. Keturah mounted the stage as everyone took a seat and began to settle down.

"As you know," she began, "our peace treaty prevents us from direct war for males. We can, however, infiltrate Femater and try to convert as many people as possible to pro-male. We ensured that there was a loophole in the treaty that allowed us to still fight for male rights as long as it included no violence of any sort."

"How do we fight for males then?" asked a woman towards the front.

"We do, of course, have a secret weapon."

"We do?" asked the same woman.

Keturah nodded. "Abel, are you here today?"

Abel stood and removed the HSD. "As you can see," Keturah continued, "we have actual contact with a male, something that no one has had for over two hundred years. We were all led under the false pretenses and propaganda that all men were evil, violent killers and that we were better off without them. Does he look like an evil, violent killer? Does he look like anything that the government has tried to project at us? We have been living off of the government's projections! But it isn't real. None of it is real. Abel," she paused to glance over at him, "Abel is real."

There were murmurs of agreement throughout the audience. Abel cleared his throat to speak. "I may not have ever left my room until the last couple weeks, but I've gotten a pretty good idea of the indoctrination of children, lies of government, and the slandering of media. It's not fair. It's not fair to me and it's not fair to all those that are being lied to. From what I've been able to see, not many people actually look happy. Not many people even interact with their families. A family is defined as a group of people who care deeply about each other no matter what, people who'd do anything for each other. Now who here can raise their hand and say honestly that they have that?"

Abel watched as a few people hesitantly raised their hands. Abel raised his and he watched as his mother and Harley did the same, Harley's eyes never leaving his. Abel did a quick count. "Twenty out of everyone here. Wow. No one else feels as though they have people who care about them unconditionally. That's so sad. What purpose of life do you have without love? Whether it is from a friend, a mother, a family member, coworker...a father...."

"Father?"

"A father is normally the eldest male's role in a family," Abel explained. "He raises the children alongside the mother. The male parent, the paternal protector and provider."

Abel shook his head and sat back down. Harley took his hand in hers. The action surprised Abel, but he didn't yank away. Harley gave his hand a light squeeze and smiled at him. Abel found it hard to concentrate on whatever Keturah was preaching now. All he could see was Harley's smile, all he could feel was her small hand in his large one, all he could hear was his heart pounding in his throat.

The meeting zoomed by with Harley's hand in his. Keturah talked about plans of "attack" and infiltration and spies and other things like that. Something about getting a bunch of people involved with the government on our side. Abel wasn't exactly paying attention.

At the end, Abel's mother stood and led the way out with Abel and Harley still hand in hand. Right before they reached the top of the stairs, Harley gasped and tugged on Abel's arm.

"What?"

"The HSD! Turn it on!"

Abel quickly turned on the device with a start, fumbling it around a little, dropping Harley's hand in the process. They ascended the last few steps and entered the discreet forest location. Harley gasped upon seeing how low the sun was. "I have to get home before Hillary does!"

She ran off through the forest, leaving Abel and his mother by themselves. "I know that you've been sneaking out again," Abel's mom finally said. Abel sucked in a sharp breath. Here it comes, he thought. "I figured since I can't seem to stop you, I might as well help you."

Abel gaped at his mother. "What?"

"Well, I can't very well let you run around without knowing you're safe."

Abel frowned, not sure whether he heard correctly or not. "Are you serious?"

"I'm dead serious, Abel. Let's start with a few basic security things. First, you have to be careful about where you go. Nothing government related and nothing with monitoring like houses. I know Harley's very skilled and is able to delete footage and make it look natural, but it's a big risk. If she makes a mistake, it's game over. You can't give out any personal information because it'll make people suspicious. Also, you can't let anyone know that you're related to me in any way. They can never trace you back to me because I've had my fair share of suspicious activity and they might figure out what's actually going on."

"I never really talk to anyone anyway. Just Harley. And she's really good at covering up for me. She's really good at most things."

Abel's mom gave him an appraising look. "Also, you shouldn't bring anything with you on your little excursions. Especially nothing traceable. And you absolutely should never, under any circumstances, reveal any plans, any people involved, and any facts. Nothing."

Sarah glanced up and down the street to make sure no one was watching and quickly ushered Abel inside. She quickly closed all the windows and deleted the security footage. "You want to eat dinner up here tonight?" Abel's mom asked.

Abel opened and closed his mouth before allowing a huge grin to spread across his face. "I'd love to."

CHAPTER 19

When Abel's mom came down the next morning to say goodbye to him and give him his breakfast, she warned him again about being careful.

"I know, Mom. I'll be careful."

Sarah kissed his forehead and left for work. Abel waited for Harley, so he could tell her the good news.

Harley poked her head through Abel's door a few minutes later. "Hey, let's hit it."

"My mom knows about us sneaking out," Abel said.

Harley's smile fell. "What—what do you mean? She can't know...she'll stop us...."

"She said that she's okay with it," Abel revealed with a smile. "She gave us her blessing."

Harley glared at Abel and walked over to punch his shoulder.

"Ow!"

"You jerk! You made me think that...that...."

"What?" Abel teased.

"That I'd never get to see you again..."

"Well, you can and you will because I'm going to annoy you for a long, long time."

"What's with all this joking around lately? Grow a funny bone finally?"

"I've been hanging out with you too much," Abel accused.

Harley grinned. "There's no such thing as too much Harley," she said. "I'm awesome."

Abel shook his head and laughed. Harley smiled at Abel and said suddenly, "Why don't we stay in again today?"

Abel nodded in agreement and smiled at her. "I can totally beat you at Sorry."

"No way. I'm totally winning," Harley argued.

They both rushed upstairs and pulled out the board game, setting it up and bantering back and forth.

They were still playing when Abel's mom got home. Harley had won fifteen times and Abel had won five times.

"Can I join?" asked Sarah.

"Sure thing, Mrs. Williams," Harley said. "Abel's losing really badly anyways."

Abel shoved Harley and laughed. "Am not! You're just jealous of my awesomeness."

Sarah shook her head and laughed at the two's childish behavior. "We'll see," said Abel's mom. "Set it up again, Harley."

Harley won *again*.... Abel refused to admit that he was actually really bad at board games. He enjoyed watching Harley laugh and do her victory dance and then brag about how amazing she was, her hair bouncing softly.

Harley had to leave soon after, but Abel's mom said that she was welcome to come again tomorrow. Harley agreed and departed. Abel helped his mom clean up the board games and Mrs. Williams made dinner.

"So...." Sarah prodded.

"What?" Abel asked as he stuffed a piece of broccoli into his mouth.

"You like Harley...."

"Mom, of course I like Harley. She's my friend," Abel scoffed as he rolled his eyes.

"I meant as more than a friend."

Abel had never really thought about this before. Harley had always been categorized as "friend" in his mind. Maybe he did like her.... When she laughed, it made Abel's heart soar and when she was sad, it made Abel want to destroy whatever had made her upset. When she held his hand, he couldn't breathe and when she smiled, he couldn't think. Abel didn't know what that meant. He had never experienced feelings like this before, but he had also never experienced friendship. Was that what friendship was like?

"Don't be ridiculous, Mom," Abel said after a few minutes of silence.

Abel's mom gave him a knowing smile and went back to munching on her salad. After dinner, Abel went back to his room and read one of Mom's really old books. *Pride and Prejudice* was so timeworn that the pages were yellowed and crackling, threatening to fall apart any second. Abel's mother had told him that it was handed down throughout the generations. It was a love story. Abel needed to know more about love. Abel needed to know what he felt.

CHAPTER 20

When Abel woke up, he realized something. When he was about seven, he had tried to sneak out. His mother had caught him before he could get anywhere far. Abel had disguised himself as well as a seven-year-old could, but that probably meant nothing. Right as Sarah was about to pull him back inside, Abel met eyes with a little girl across the street. Her blonde hair was in messy curls, flying in every direction and her blue eyes shone with defiance as a girl that looked to be about thirteen tried to yank her down the street.

"Come on, Harl," the older one pleaded. "We have to go to school."

"You can't tell me what to do, Hill," the little girl argued. She made eye contact with Abel and offered him a small, almost wicked smile. And then she winked. Like she *knew*.

Just as the older one was about to glance in Abel's direction, the little girl stopped fighting and raced ahead of who Abel had assumed was her sister. "Harley!" the older girl called. "Harley, get back here!"

"Which do you want, Hillary? Go to school or stay back there?" the little girl taunted as she continued to race ahead of her sister.

Abel had met Harley before. And she had protected him then, too. Abel wondered if Harley remembered this or if she even correlated it back to Abel.

He couldn't believe it had taken him this long to make the connections.

Abel heard voices upstairs. One was his mother for sure, but the other one he couldn't quite place.

"Yes, Mrs. Williams. I told her that I'd forget about it, but I saw her leaving your house again yesterday."

"It's fine Hillary. I invited Harley. I'm mentoring her."

"Why didn't she just tell me that? Why did she lie to   me?"

"She didn't want anyone to know. Harley's very independent, you know. Hates having to admit that she needs help sometimes."

"I know what you mean, Sarah. Well, thank you for your time."

Abel was surprised by his mother's quick and smooth lies. Had he been Hillary, he wouldn't've given it a second thought. A third voice entered the mix.

"Hillary? What are you doing here?" asked Harley.

"I saw you leave Mrs. Williams's house yesterday and I informed her of my suspicions."

"And I was just telling her about how I was mentoring you," Sarah quickly added.

There was a moment of silence before Harley said in an indignant voice, "You told her? We agreed that no one should know!"

"I didn't see any other choice," Abel's mom said. "She was going to report you for a felony."

"Thanks for your time, Sarah. See you at work tomorrow."

"Bye, Hillary. We had better get down to business, Harley."

The front door opened and shut again. "Thanks, Mrs. Williams," Harley breathed. "That was close."

"Well, I guess I'm staying home from work today. Hillary thinks I'm mentoring you. Go get Abel then."

Abel could hear Harley walking downstairs and began to panic. He couldn't even understand why. It was just Harley. The memory had triggered something inside of Abel.

Harley opened his door and smiled at him. The knot in his chest relaxed slightly and was replaced by a childlike giddiness. "Did you hear all of that?"

Abel nodded and tried to swallow the lump that was obstructing his throat.

"Well, come on. I have officially challenged you to another board game war."

She was just about to turn around again when a small gasp escaped her lips and she beelined for Abel's desk. "Where'd you get this?" she marveled.

Heat rose into Abel's cheeks. In her hands, Harley held his copy of *Pride and Prejudice*.

"It was my mom's, I suppose," Abel muttered, snatching it out of her hands.

"But...but how'd she get it?"

"What do you mean?" Abel asked.

Harley raised an eyebrow at him. "Books...they aren't really banned...but they basically don't exist anymore. Something about conserving trees, blah, blah, blah, but really they just want to get rid of everything BME because, well, I guess, that some books portray males in a positive manner."

He didn't answer her; Abel was still embarrassed at the book she had found.

He stood and followed Harley upstairs. He still couldn't manage to choke out any words. How had he not noticed her pure beauty before? She was so amazing in every way possible.

Abel's mom was waiting with a stack of board games next to her and Harley took the seat across from her. Abel sat next to Harley and tried to clear his throat.

"What game first, Abel?" asked Harley.

Abel said the first thing that came to mind. "Scr-scrabble."

How appropriate. A game about making words seeing as Abel couldn't seem to form any of his own.

Harley didn't comment at his obvious stutter, but his mother sent Abel a smirk.

"That's a thirty-point word!" Harley cheered. "I win!"

Abel laughed as she did her signature happy dance complete with singing. "Go Harley, go Harley. You're so awesome, you're so awesome. Way better than Abel, way better than Abel!"

Abel's mom couldn't help but laugh as too and soon they were all singing Harley's victory song and dancing her victory dance. Abel was doing in more of a mocking manner and Harley grabbed a throw pillow off the couch and smacked him over the head with it. Abel raised his eyebrows at Harley and grabbed a different pillow, smacking her across the face with it.

Harley gasped and hit Abel again and Abel retaliated. They were having a full-blown pillow fight within seconds with Abel's mom laughing at them in the background. Harley tackled Abel and began to beat him with her pillow. "Resistance is futile!" she yelled.

In all honesty, Abel could have easily turned the situation around, but he was laughing too hard and he loved seeing Harley so happy. When he had finally managed to stop laughing long enough to take a breath, he flipped over and flung Harley over his back jumping up and down slightly so she thumped against his back. Then he began to spin in circles to make her dizzy. Finally, he let her slide off and catch her breath. She stayed on the floor, letting her laughter die out slowly and smiling like a lunatic.

Abel was grinning as well and Abel's mother was laughing at the two children. When they had all finally settled down, Abel helped Harley up off the ground and shook his head. "Who's the winner now?"

"Still me," she said, slapping his arm.

Abel stuck his tongue out at her and crossed his arms. Harley shook her head with a laugh. "Such a baby," she teased.

"Such an annoyance," he responded.

Harley slapped his arm again as they sat back down at the table. "If I give you a rematch, will you shut up?"

Abel pretended to ponder this. "Probably not," he declined.

"That's because I'll just win again," Harley sang.

"You're on!"

Abel's mom set up another game of Scrabble. And Harley won....

Again....

"You cheat," Abel accused.

Harley faked a gasp. "How did you know?"

"So you admit! Aha! I win by default!"

"Sarcasm, Abel, dearest. It is called sarcasm."

"Whatever," Abel grumbled. "It's getting late, actually," he said, glancing at the clock. "You should probably get going, Harley."

"I'll be back tomorrow and I expect you to up your game."

"Whatever," Abel repeated. "We're going out tomorrow."

"Can't stand another loss, eh?"

"Can't stand another day trapped in this house with you."

"As opposed to being trapped outside the house with me?" Harley questioned with a raised eyebrow.

"Pretty much," Abel agreed.

"Yeah, whatever you say, Abel. You're just a sore loser."

"Exactly," Abel admitted.

Harley laughed and left Abel and his mother alone again.

"Yeah, you don't like her at all...." Abel's mom said sarcastically with a smirk.

Abel glared at her. "I'll be going to my room now."

Her laughter followed him all the way down the hall, down the staircase, and into his room.

Abel sat up late that night, finishing *Pride and Prejudice*. Maybe he did like Harley....

Maybe....

He liked Harley.

CHAPTER 21

Abel and Harley left early that morning. Sarah had made them a picnic that they were going to eat at the clearing. Harley didn't talk the whole way there which was highly unsettling since all she ever did was talk and joke and laugh. She wasn't even smiling. Not very Harley-like at all.

Abel tried to make conversation with her. "My mom almost put a board game in with the picnic."

"That's nice," Harley answered distractedly.

"I was thinking about jumping off the cliff when we get there," Abel tested.

"That's a great idea," Harley agreed.

Abel sighed and fell silent again, letting her lead through the dense foliage. When they reached the clearing, Abel spread the blanket out and placed the food on it. "What's up with you today, Harley? You aren't acting like yourself."

Harley finally met Abel's eyes for the first time that day. They were red-rimmed and puffy. She had been crying.

"What happened?" Abel asked, feeling rage build up inside of him. "Who did this to you?"

Harley shook her head over and over again, tears springing back into her eyes. "No one did it to me, Abel. I guess you can say that I did this to myself."

"What's wrong, Harley? Let me help you the way you helped me."

Harley shook her head again. "You already have, Abel. You've helped me more than I ever thought was possible."

It was Abel's turn to shake his head. "I haven't done anything for you."

"You saved me. You saved me from myself."

"I think you're confused, Harley. *You* saved *me*. I haven't done anything."

"Abel, I was going to—to kill myself the day I met you. There wasn't any point to my life. No one cared about me and no one loved me and I absolutely hated my life, my situation. I hated that I couldn't do anything to change anything. I had no purpose...and then I bumped into you. You gave me purpose, Abel, you cared about me.

"You know that robot that you destroyed? It was built and sent by another student. They *hate* me. And I was going to let it hurt me too. But at the last second I chickened out and screamed."

"But why are you upset right now? What's wrong now?"

Harley began shaking her head again and Abel cupped his hands to her cheeks. "Harley, you can tell me anything, okay?"

Tears began to leak out of her eyes. "I think Hillary is onto us. I think she's connecting the dots and if she finds out about you, she won't hesitate; she'll call the authorities and you'll be murdered. I can't—I can't lose you, Abel."

"Listen to me. You are the single most amazing person I've ever met; don't you ever forget that. Even if I'm gone, even if I'm dead, never forget that and never, ever think that you aren't worth anything or that no one cares. It isn't true."

Abel wrapped his arms around Harley and she wept into his shoulder. "You saved me too, Harley. We saved each other, but most of all we cared about each other. You are marvelous, miraculous, and phenomenal."

Harley laughed into Abel's shoulder, coming out as a muffled giggle. "Now let's eat," Abel said, trying to lighten the mood. "I'm starving; all these emotions are exhausting."

Harley shook her head; Abel thought she might give herself whiplash. "Why do I put up with you, Abel?"

"Shoot if I know. Something about me saving you and caring about you, blah, blah, blah. That spaghetti smells really good."

Harley hit Abel's arm and flung some of the aforementioned spaghetti at him. "Jerk."

"Stupid."

"Bozo."

"Idiot."

"Dummy."

"You're great."

"You're great, too. You're catching on to this teasing thing."

"I learn from the best," Abel said while stuffing some spaghetti into his face.

Harley took a piece of bread and wiped off some of the marinara sauce that had smeared above Abel's eyebrow. "Your mom makes really good spaghetti."

"Well, she's one of the only ones that still believe in actual cooking. Everyone else uses those instant meal things. 'Just add water and heat' or whatever." Harley nodded.

"So what about your mother?" Abel asked. "I've only ever seen Hillary. Does she just never leave the house like me or is she always out of the house or have I just never seen her?"

Harley glared at the ground. "My mother was arrested for treason against the government. She was trying to prove that not all males were evil just like not all women are good. The government didn't like that. She's been rotting in a cell ever since. Hillary has tried to cover up and 'do better', but I've embraced her beliefs wholeheartedly. She was right."

"I'd like to meet her one day," Abel said. "Do you have visitation rights?"

Harley shook her head. "Hillary does, but I think she'd rather say that she was never associated with our mom. When I turn eighteen, I'll be able to. She was arrested when I was eight. Do you think she'd even recognize me?"

"Of course. She'd hear one word out of your mouth and know that it was her headstrong Harley coming to bust her out."

Harley nudged her elbow into Abel's ribs and laughed. "I just wish it wasn't like this."

Abel wrapped an arm around Harley's shoulders. "Things will be different soon," he promised.

Harley rested her head on Abel's shoulder and gave a small smile. "It already is, Abel. You've changed everything."

And in that moment Abel knew. He liked Harley.

CHAPTER 22

Harley and Abel were walking next to the river the next day. Harley had shown it to Abel a while back and he had simply fallen in love with the scene. It was a rapid flowing river, about twenty feet wide and maybe twenty feet deep at the deepest point. Abel loved the smooth stones that appeared at the edges of the water banks.

Harley was telling Abel some story about when she was five and nearly set her house on fire. It only made Abel think of the day when he was seven and saw Harley for the first time. Harley fell silent all of a sudden.

"What is it?" Abel asked.

"Shush," she hissed. She pulled Abel behind a bush and pushed his head down. "Stay low and turn the HSD back on."

Abel had gotten into the habit of turning it off whenever they were in a secluded area. He clicked it back on and strained his ears to listen to whatever Harley had heard. Leaves crackled and twigs snapped and there was the low hum of something else that Abel didn't recognize.

A huge metal contraption with wheels rolled up to the riverbank. "What is that thing?" Abel whispered.

"It's a truck. Self-driving truck. Not many people have those," Harley answered.

On the side, the letters, **BDU**, were inscribed. "What does 'BDU' stand for?" Abel wondered.

Harley shrugged. "Stay here," she instructed. "I'm going to get closer."

"No way," Abel said. "I'm coming with you."

Harley sighed and shook her head. "It's probably a government vehicle. Too risky."

Abel was about to object, but the truck door opened and Harley scampered off before Abel could do anything stupid. He watched as Harley darted from bush to bush. The woman who had stepped out of the truck looked about thirty. She was wearing a uniform that was all blue and had the same letters inscribed on it.

The lady walked around to the back of the truck and pulled out a huge black bag that was about double—maybe triple—the size of the woman herself. As she heaved the large bag over her shoulder and trekked towards the river, a small hole ripped at the bottom and what appeared to be a tiny arm revealed itself.

Abel could hear Harley swearing from where he was. Her gasp echoed across the forest and the lady turned to face where Harley was hidden. Not that she needed too; Harley was storming up to the lady, looking livid and disgusted.

"What do you think you're doing?!" Harley screamed.

"Transporting goods," the lady answered monotonously.

"If by goods, you mean dead *babies*!" Harley screeched.

"Look, kid, I'm just doing my job. They tell me to take the bag to the river, so I take the bag to the river."

"That's a lie and you know it!"

"Kid, this is some pretty big stuff you're messing with. If you leave now, I'll forget you were ever here."

"The government is killing babies," Harley gasped. "That's disgusting; that's horrendous."

"What do you want me to do, kid? I'm just a worker. I don't have any say."

"You could protest, go on strike! You could bring this to the public eye! You could do so much and yet when they tell you to dispose of the babies they murdered, you say 'okay boss' and take the bag to the river!"

"It's not that simple, kid. They've threatened my family. If anyone finds out, they'll take my children, my sisters and their children, my mother."

"Why? Why are they doing this?" Harley whispered. She sounded close to tears.

"Overpopulation. They already put a restriction on the amount of kids you can have. You have to have authorization to give birth, so they can control how many babies are born, but it still wasn't enough. Now whenever mothers take their kids to the doctor, the government orders that the doctors tell the moms that their kids are gravely ill and then kill the children."

Harley fell to her knees and a loud sob escaped her lips. Abel had to resist the urge to run forward and wrap her in his arms. "Listen, you can't tell anyone, kid. They'll get me and my family."

Harley shook her head and tears streamed down her face. Abel couldn't take it anymore. He rushed from his spot behind his bush and wrapped his arms around Harley. She buried her head in his shoulder and sobbed. Abel glared at the woman. "You make me sick," he growled.

Harley hiccuped and wiped under her eyes. "Abel," she whispered, "your voice."

"I don't even care anymore, Harley."

"Lady," Abel said, "I have a proposition for you. Every Monday a secret group of abolitionists meets. I want you to come and share your information. No one will ever know. And if you don't, if you tell anyone about the meeting, I'll tell everyone about what the government is doing and make sure they know where I got my information."

The woman nodded and stayed silent. She seemed to be pondering Abel's voice and his aggression. While Harley sobbed next to him, he was threatening the woman, borderline blackmailing. Maybe men were more aggressive than women, but for good reason.

Abel pulled Harley up. "You never saw us," Abel told the woman.

He let Harley lean on him as she cried and he led them to the clearing so that they could be alone. Abel turned off the HSD and let Harley weep into him. He stroked her hair and held her. "It's going to be okay," he promised.

"How can you say that?" Harley sniffled.

"Well, that's what we're doing, isn't it? Making a difference. She's coming to the meeting and she's going to inform us on all the goings that no one knows about."

Harley met Abel's eyes. "You really think we're making a difference?"

"I know so."

Harley dried her eyes with her sleeve and took Abel's hand. "How are you so good at this?"

"At what?"

"Everything. Making me feel better, making a difference, being a good person, doing the right thing, saying the right thing."

Abel shrugged. "I guess I'm not. I just try to be."

Harley shook her head. "How poetic," she scoffed. "Come on; let's get home."

CHAPTER 23

When Harley got home, the lights were off. But she knew someone was there; she could sense it. You know that feeling of emptiness a house gets when one of your family members is gone? The absence of their presence. And you can just feel the difference in the air. That's how Harley knew.

She walked carefully into the kitchen. Empty. Harley snuck down the hallway and just as she was about to step into her room, she noticed the light on in her mother's room. It hadn't been stepped into since her mother went to jail.

She stepped through the threshold and saw Hillary sitting on the bed. "Hillary?" Harley questioned. "What are you doing in here?"

Hillary didn't answer, but she turned to face Harley. "I didn't want to do this."

"Do what? Hillary, you aren't acting normal. You're starting to scare me."

"Harley, don't lie to me. I know that you aren't being mentored by Sarah. I don't know why she's covering up for you, but something isn't right. I'm not stupid. Now I am only going to ask you once: what are you doing?"

"I don't know what you're talking about." The words sounded feeble, even to Harley.

"Don't lie to me!" Hillary screeched. "You don't understand, Harley. You're too young and ignorant. I've had to raise you, provide for you, and work past the reputation Mom had labeled us with. Don't you dare lie to me!"

"Hillary, you think I'm young and stupid, but I'm not! I used to spend every day trying to be your friend, but you weren't having it. I reminded you of Mom, so you automatically hated me. I'm not lying." Her voice sounded stronger this time, more sure.

Before Harley could even react, she was on the ground and there was a sharp stinging in her cheek. Surprise overrode the pain. Harley didn't cry, but she felt almost...embarrassed. It was ridiculous because it should be the hitter that felt ashamed, but Harley was embarrassed and surprised and the thing that hurt the most was that Hillary would actually hit her own sister.

"I said don't lie to me!" Hillary seethed.

Harley stood up off the floor and narrowed her eyes at Hillary. She could already feel one of them swelling shut. Before anyone could do anything, Harley pushed Hillary to the ground and ran into her room, locking the door.

As soon as she was behind closed doors, the tears came freely. Crying made her feel weak, but she couldn't help it. Harley knew that she couldn't stay here anymore. She had to run away whether Abel would come with her or not.

Her mind was clouded and she felt drowsy all of a sudden. Harley had read somewhere that you weren't supposed to sleep after a head injury, but she couldn't help but let her eyes slip shut and she fell asleep, laying on the ground next to her door.

CHAPTER 24

Abel was eating breakfast upstairs with his mother when Harley burst in. Her hair hung loosely around her face so that Abel couldn't see her eyes. "Harley," Abel's mom greeted, "you're here early."

"Have some breakfast," Abel offered.

Harley looked up and Abel dropped his fork. Her eye was swollen shut and was all black and blue. Abel rushed forward and cupped her face in his hands. "What happened? Who did this?"

Harley opened her mouth, but all that came out was a weak sob. "I have to go, Abel. I can't stay with her anymore. I have to go."

"Hillary did this to you?"

Harley nodded her head. Sarah gasped from behind Abel. "I came to say goodbye."

"No," Abel whispered to himself. "No, you can't leave me. Stay here. Hide in the basement with me."

Abel felt extremely selfish for asking her not to leave, but Harley's eyes lit up. "Really? Is that okay with you, Sarah?"

"I don't see why not," Abel's mom said with an approving nod. "Let's go get your things then."

Harley nodded. "Hillary already left."

Abel ran downstairs and grabbed the HSD, turning it on and sprinting back upstairs. "Let's go," he said to his mom and Harley.

Abel took Harley's hand and let his mom lead the way to Harley's house. When they arrived, Harley let Abel's hand slip from her own and opened the front door. She walked inside and went straight to her room, grabbing a few things and shoving them into a bag. Abel turned off the HSD and sat down on Harley's bed. She scurried around her room, grabbing clothes out of drawers, notebooks out of drawers.

Her room was pretty empty as it was. There was a loud slamming noise and Abel jumped up. Harley fretfully looked at the door, dread filling her expression. Sarah came running in. "Abel, quick—"

Hillary walked into Harley's room. Anger filled Abel's veins. He forgot everything: boy, girl, revolutions, illegality. He just wanted to do something, anything to this woman who had hurt Harley.

Hillary stood in the doorway for a moment with her mouth agape before she composed herself. "Now I see. Sneaking around with an illegal male, huh, Harley? And you, Sarah, harboring him. Is he yours? Oh my god...."

"Hillary," Harley tried to reason with evident panic in her voice, "let me explain."

"You know what's really funny about all of this, though," Hillary said with a laugh that was anything but happy or amused, "I suspected this. I kept telling myself that I was being paranoid because of Mom, but it turns out that I was right."

"Hillary, stop. Stop and be logical," Harley explained. "You're smart. You must understand that what the government is doing is wrong."

Hillary shook her head and pressed a button that was on her wall. It crackled slightly and Hillary said, "We have a code IM1: Red. Location: 6692348, activation code: H9432CJ."

Harley glared at her sister. "You are despicable. I hope you realize that you've just murdered Abel."

"So it has a name?"

"Yes, 'it' does," Abel growled. "You know nothing about me or any other male."

Hillary narrowed her eyes. "I know that males are liars and smooth talkers and they have the ability to persuade people into doing whatever they say."

Hillary turned to Sarah. "I respected you," she spat.

Sarah's red-rimmed eyes narrowed. "And that is something that I would gladly give up."

There were loud bangs from outside and Abel realized something: he was about to die. His brain couldn't quite process that. It didn't feel real. Numbness washed over him and he sat down. He felt like he was about to throw up.

Three women stormed inside. "Hillary, where's the male?"

Hillary pointed at Abel with a twisted smile on her face.

"To the backyard," the first woman ordered.

She jabbed the muzzle of her rifle into Abel's back and he marched forward and out the back door with the other two women, Hillary, Sarah, and Harley behind him. "On your knees, hands behind your head," the woman barked.

Abel got onto his knees and placed his hands behind his head. Harley rushed to his side. "Out of the way, girl," one of the other women ordered.

Harley glared at her. "I want to be with him when he dies," she said through clenched teeth.

Harley stood up and took a few steps forward. Sarah was sobbing behind Hillary and the first woman shrugged. "Suit yourself, girl."

Abel closed his eyes. It seemed as though if the bullet didn't kill him, the lack of oxygen would. His chest was tight, but he felt...resigned.

"One," the first women shouted.

Abel sucked in a sharp breath.

"Two."

The only noise was his mother's sobs.

"Three."

A loud bang echoed across the entire neighborhood and Harley screamed, "NO!" Too quickly for anyone to react, Harley had jumped in front of Abel and lay on the ground in front of him.

CHAPTER 25

A deep red spot flourished through her white shirt and Harley pressed her hand to the wound. It was in her lower abdomen and Harley's face immediately turned ghostly white.

"Oh my god," Hillary whispered.

Abel rushed over to Harley's side. "Harley! Harley, no!"

He pressed his hands into the wound, trying to prevent more loss of blood. Harley let out a hiss of pain. "Abel, it's okay."

"How can you say that? It isn't okay!"

"Shush," she whispered. Her voice was hoarse.

"You can't do this to me, Harley. You weren't supposed to—this wasn't—you can't..."

Sarah was at Abel's side. She kneeled beside him and silent tears fell down her cheeks. "Harley...."

Abel felt his own eyes prick with tears. "There's so much I have to say, to learn, so much for you to teach me. Harley, you can't leave me yet."

"Abel, I...need...to...tell you.... You...."

Her face went slack and her eyes rolled back into her head. Harley's whole body began convulsing and then went completely still again. "Harley! Harley, no!" Abel sobbed, pulling her body close to his own. "Harley, come back. I love you! Harley...."

The three women sent to execute Abel were all lying on the ground too. Hillary had knocked them all out.

"Harley," Abel begged, "don't go."

Hillary was sobbing and fell to her knees. "This wasn't supposed to happen," she cried.

"This is all your fault!" Abel screamed. He had never felt so angry in his entire life. Blood roared through his ears and adrenaline rushed through his veins. All he could see was Harley's lifeless body and all he wanted to see was her shining smile.

Hillary nodded. "I know," she sobbed.

Abel laid Harley's body back down and closed her eyes. Sarah felt for a pulse and pulled her fingers away, closing her eyes.

Abel couldn't think. It didn't feel real. It felt like Harley would open her eyes and smile, laughing at Abel's belief that she was dead, mocking him for believing her act. But it wasn't an act and Harley wouldn't open her eyes.

Abel looked at his shaking hands. They were covered in blood. Her blood. Abel's eyes blurred and he couldn't breathe.

Hillary looked up at Abel. "You have to go," she said finally. "You have to hide. I'll tell everyone that it was a false alarm and that they shot Harley under the mistaken belief that she was the illegal male. You have to go."

Abel couldn't move, but his mother pulled him up. "Go to the clearing," she instructed. "Wait for me there. Do *not* take off the HSD."

Abel nodded numbly, stumbling away from the backyard. His movements felt sluggish, like he was trying to swim through molasses.

Eventually he got his limbs to move and began to run to the clearing. When he got there, he sat on a rock and held his head between his hands. Numb. That was all he felt. The whole area surrounding him was filled with memories of Harley. Memories were all they were now.

Numb.

It didn't feel real. He didn't want it to be real. His brain seemed to stop functioning and he couldn't think at all. Time ticked by agonizingly slowly, waiting for his mother. Waiting.

Numb.

A twig snapping echoed through the forest. Abel slowly lifted his head to see what it was. His mother came crashing through the bushes, panting and still covered in blood. Harley's blood.

"You can't go back to the house," Sarah said as soon as she saw Abel. "You have to hide in the meeting hall. I'll bring you your things. It isn't safe for you to go back to the house."

Abel didn't answer; he just nodded and began to walk in the direction of the meeting hall. Harley was the one who had originally brought him there. Abel tried to remember what day of the week it was. Thursday? Friday? He was pretty sure that it was Friday.

The gears in Abel's head began turning. He couldn't let Harley have died for nothing. If he wasn't serious about the male rights movement before, he sure was now. A plan formulated itself in his head and he couldn't help but think about what Harley would've said.

His mom cleared her throat from behind him and Abel jumped slightly. "Are you okay?"

"I'm fine."

"I know how difficult this must be for you—"

"I'm *fine*, Mom! Okay? I'm fine," Abel snapped.

His mom cast him a worried look, but Abel ignored it and continued trudging through the forest. It didn't take long to get to the meeting hall from where they were and Abel opened the secret staircase and descended into the long hallway that let out into the circular room. Inside was only Keturah. Abel wondered if she lived here too.

Keturah glanced up from whatever she was reading and saw Abel. "To what do I owe the pleasure?"

"Abel needs a place to stay," Sarah explained. "He's been discovered and we have to hide him."

If Keturah noticed the blood all over Abel, she didn't comment. "You can stay here," Keturah said with a nod. "The only people that know about this place are the people that come to the meetings."

Abel sat down in one of the chairs and sighed. "I'll be right back with some of your things," Sarah said. "You need some fresh clothes to change into."

She gave Abel one last sad grimace and walked back down the hallway, leaving him with Keturah.

"What happened?" she asked.

Abel shook his head and glared at the ground. "I don't want to talk about it."

"Talking usually makes you feel better," Keturah offered.

That sounded like something Harley would say. Abel stood, knocking over his chair in the process. "I said I don't want to talk about it, okay?!"

He kicked the chair that had fallen over. It jumped about ten feet away, knocking over three more in the process. Abel kicked the nearest chair, sending it flying. His chest heaved with rage; his breathing was ragged and heavy.

Keturah gave him a pitiful look and sat down on the floor. "Sometimes life seems cruel," she said. Abel waited for her to finish, but she didn't continue.

"But..." he prompted.

"There is no but. That's it. Sometimes life seems cruel. And it is. But courage is being able to stand up and say that even though you're scared, hurt, upset, angry you're going to continue fighting to make things better."

"Thanks," Abel muttered. "I feel so much better."

"That wasn't supposed to make you feel better. It was me telling you to, as they said BME, 'man up' and deal with it."

"Thanks. That's so much better," he grumbled.

Keturah shrugged. "Not everything is meant to make you feel better."

A few moments later, Abel's mother returned, holding a backpack and something that smelled suspiciously like chocolate.

"Hey, sweetie," she whispered, setting down her things and sitting next to Abel. She leaned over and kissed his forehead. "I brought you some clothes, some notebooks, a few things to pass the time, and chocolate cake."

"Thanks, mom," Abel muttered, running his blood-caked hands through his hair.

"Is there anywhere he can shower?" Sarah asked Keturah.

"Sure. There's emergency commons out that door. Bedrooms and bathrooms."

Abel had never noticed another door before, but now that he was looking, he could see the large oak door that Keturah had pointed to. Abel stood and wandered through the door, walking down a short hallway that turned into a room with a few couches and chairs and a fireplace. On the left and right of the room, there were two more doors.

Abel poked his head through the door to the left and found himself in a large room with about ten bunkbeds. He walked to the opposite side of the room and opened the door on the right to find a bathroom with about five shower stalls and five toilet stalls with a wall lined with sinks. To the very back, there was a row of cabinets. Abel opened one and found it stocked with towels; he opened another and found soap and toilet paper. He continued down the row of cabinets until he had all the supplies necessary for a shower.

He stepped into the first shower stall and turned the water all the way up to hot and let it wash over him, cleansing him of the day's events. He stood there for a good hour, letting his mind go numb and letting his body relax.

When he finally got out, the entire room was filled with steam and the humidity was suffocating. He quickly dressed and padded over to the bedroom area. He found that his mother had set his backpack and cake on the first bed.

Abel stuffed the chocolate into his face and when he had finished, he collapsed onto the bottom bunk. Exhaustion swept over him and he gave in, drifting off into a dreamless sleep.

CHAPTER 26

When Abel woke up, he was disoriented by his surroundings. This wasn't his basement. Then, the previous day's events came crashing into his brain like a tsunami. His chest constricted and he couldn't breathe. *Boom*!

The gunshot echoed in his head.

Harley was gone.

He sat up and rested his head in the palms of his hands. He wondered if anyone else was there. It was a Saturday which meant his mother wouldn't be at work. Another thought occurred to him: how was he supposed to get sustenance?

Abel shook his head, sending all of his thoughts swirling away into his subconscious abyss. He stood and walked to the circular room to see if anyone was there. Empty. He checked the bathrooms and the living room area. Nobody.

Abel sighed and sat back down on his bed. He was confused as to what he was supposed to do for breakfast. His stomach was already rumbling and he was bored.

You would think that after eighteen years of living in a basement he would have a high boredom tolerance, but no. If anything, he had an unusually small boredom tolerance. Abel began to dig through the bag his mother had packed. He hadn't actually looked at it except to grab a pair of clothes last night.

He found several changes of clothes, a notebook, a few books (old fashioned but not traceable), and a few granola bars. Abel grabbed one and stuffed it into his mouth, trying to ease the hunger pains in his upper abdomen.

As he sat in silence, the scene of Harley's death played over and over in his mind as though his own brain was trying to torture him even further. Everything else drowned away as the moment was relived. He didn't remember standing up, but he managed to trip over the bed post and face plant onto the floor.

If Harley were there, she would have been laughing so hard she was snorting.

Harley.

Abel heard a few noises from the main room and he emerged from the commons. Sarah was standing in the center of the circular room. "I brought you breakfast," she said, offering Abel a bag.

Abel accepted gratefully and began shoveling the food into his mouth. "So I know that this is probably really difficult for you right now, but wounds heal with time."

Abel glared at his mother. "I'm freaking fine, Mom! I don't want to sit down and talk about my feelings for hours on end. I don't want to sit here and mourn. I don't want to *think*. I just want to make a change the way *she* wanted."

Sarah frowned. "It isn't healthy to bottle up emotions, Abel."

"I'm not bottling anything. Just leave me alone about this, okay? Talking about it isn't going to change anything."

Abel's mom sighed, but didn't press the matter further. She sat with Abel for about another hour before leaving him by himself again.

Abel walked back to the bedroom and pulled out the notebook, formulating a plan.

Plan for Success

Go to press

Write anonymous articles in news

Gain support

Slowly leak information about the government to turn people against them

Invade the government; make them see that men aren't evil

Overthrow government

Abel's master plan....

It had a few holes, but it was only the general outline....

Abel heard more noises outside and walked back into the circular room. Keturah was rushing around the room, grabbing papers and reading documents.

"What's going on?" asked Abel.

"Your mother's just told me what happened yesterday. Harley was technically a Masculumian. Masculum was never really a place, but more of a state of mind. That means that by shooting her, the government of Femater has violated their own peace treaty without even realizing it."

"So you're saying..."

"That's exactly what I'm saying. I just need to check some facts before formulating a plan. It'll be a complete surprise because they don't even know that they've violated anything."

"Is there anything I can do to help?" Abel queried.

So Keturah set him to work cross-referencing, checking, reading, and documenting. And his mind was taken off of Harley for a little while.

CHAPTER 27

The weekend ticked by agonizingly slowly again. Abel was back to square one and he was so tired of it. At night he couldn't sleep because of nightmares and during the day he had nothing to do except think about the nightmares of the previous night. It was a vicious cycle that was leaving Abel tired and ornery.

Sarah visited when she could and Keturah could often be found in the circular room, but Abel tended to avoid her because she always made comments about his ratty appearance and horrible attitude, often wondering aloud if all males were that way.

Monday came slower than Abel would have liked, but it was there nonetheless and the abolitionist meeting was upon him. He had planned for this all weekend and yet he still didn't know what he was going to say. The meeting room began to fill up with women and soon Keturah had called order.

She opened the meeting with the usual stuff and then motioned for Abel to take the stage. He stood and cleared his throat. "So the past week has brought some things to light for me. The first of which being that I don't want to sit in this dingy room anymore and hope for a better life; I have to make it happen. I'm tired of playing it safe and hoping for the best. I'm not going to sit around anymore. I'm not going to sneak around anymore! I'm going to do something!"

There were a few cheers of agreement. "One of you with us today is new here. We met at the river. You didn't see me like this though; you saw me in disguise. You made me a promise and I want to hold you to that. Please stand."

A woman towards the back stood up with an expression of confusion on her face. "This woman," Abel continued, "has been paid by the government to dispose of dead babies that *they've* killed."

A few gasps rang out in the room. "I have a plan to expose them for what they are doing. If the world knew what was going on, they would not be behind Femater, I can guarantee that. These are our children, our families, our communities, and our friends. If we stand together, we can overthrow the government!"

There were murmurs of agreement and a few women even began clapping. Abel hadn't really thought his speech was that special; he hadn't even planned on making a speech.

"Now I have a question for you: does anyone in here work with the newspaper?"

A different woman in the front stood. "I am an editor and publisher for *The Early Morning Chronicle*."

"I'm going to need you to publish a few things with your next article."

Abel scanned the crowd for his mother and when he spotted her, he was surprised to see who was seated next to her: Hillary.

Abel refocused his attention on the woman in front of him. "I'll give you the article that I want published after the meeting. I guess that's all I have to say," Abel wrapped up a little lamely, sitting back in his chair.

He swiveled around and briefly met Hillary's puffy eyes before turning away again. He had never noticed before how much she resembled Harley. Her blonde hair was only a few shades lighter and instead of loose curls, it fell limply against her shoulders and was usually tied up in a ponytail or a bun. Her blue eyes were grayer than Harley's and they looked more stressed. Harley always looked like she was ready to burst into laughter. It was painful to see someone so similar and yet so different, like an everlasting reminder that Harley was gone and Abel would never meet anyone like her again.

Abel didn't pay attention to the rest of the meeting. His mind was on the article that he had written the previous night. The one that he had tucked away in his pocket. He pulled it out to go over it one more time. The paper was crinkled from the amount of times he had read over it, double and triple and quadruple checking.

Surprises in Femater: Good and Bad

By: Anonymous Submitter

So I guess I should start with the fact that I am a male. I can practically hear the gasps. Many of you may just stop reading now, but I encourage you to continue. In this article I plan to bring light to a few things that I doubt you understand.

Firstly, not all males are evil just like not all women are evil. I can assure you that I am not evil (though you may not believe me, nor do I expect you to). Maybe if I describe myself, it will help you grasp this concept. For the sake of secrecy, I can't go too far into detail. I'm eighteen. I've lived in hiding my entire life up until recently.

When I first emerged from my hiding place, the world was a baffling place that I was mostly ignorant to; I was just exhilarated to be outside. My first burst of reality was when I got caught. From the time I could talk, it had been drilled into my head that if I were to go outside and be caught, it would mean certain death. I lived in fear and in exile. But I escaped.

I was caught by a young woman who is currently deceased because of me. Because she helped me. Because of the government. She died, bleeding and without her family. She protected me, taught me, and helped me. Within a few weeks, I had learned more about this cruel world than I had in my entire life. Indoctrination runs rampant through the school systems and the media; everyone is always taught the evils of men before they can even walk. But it isn't factually correct

I am not a killer, nor a rapist. I don't think lowly of women. It's almost laughable how hypocritical these preaches are. Women state that they are looked down on by men, but by doing so, they are looking down on men. Women claim all men are heartless murderers, but just last week I caught a woman disposing of dead babies' bodies on order of the government. They had been killed in secret due to overpopulation. Have you ever had a child pronounced 'suddenly ill' by the doctor only to have them not return? Who's the murderer now?

Man or woman, there is no one type of person. Everyone is unique and different. Yes, there probably were bad men BME, but there were also bad women. There still are bad women, just as, I'm sure, would be the same for men if they were still around. It isn't about gender or race or anything like *that. It's who you are and who you choose to be every day of your life. I choose to make a difference. What do you choose?*

Abel was fairly satisfied with it. When the meeting had finished, he stood and handed it to the newspaper lady. She thanked him and departed just like everyone else. Soon, Abel was left all by himself again. It seemed that he was always by himself when it boiled down to it. When Harley had been around, that wasn't the case. Abel felt furious with himself for all the self-pity. It was selfish and, quite frankly, it was annoying him.

There was nothing he could do, so why dwell on it?

All of his thoughts seemed to conflate into one jumbled mess. Even though he had only been up for a few hours, his body felt as though it had run a marathon. His mind was sluggish and desultory.

Abel slogged back to the bedroom and sat on his bed, pulling out some of the books his mother had packed. Among them was Pride and Prejudice. Abel tossed it aside and grabbed the next one, Animal Farm. Abel was fairly sure that he had never read this one before. It was seemingly short and the cover was weathered and tattered. Anything to get his mind off of, well...everything.

Abel picked it up and became immersed in the book. He was surprised by the deep plot and the beautiful symbolism. Ironically, he had picked the book up to keep him from thinking and it only made him think more. He had finished it within several hours of nonstop reading.

When he had finally emerged from his room, his mother was seated in the meeting hall with a steaming plate of food. "Hey, babe," she greeted. "Thought you might be hungry."

Abel nodded and accepted the plate.

"Lucy showed me the article you wrote."

Who was Lucy? Abel could only infer that it was the news lady. He nodded again, prompting his mother to continue.

"Don't you think it's a bit risky?"

"How so? There is no possible way that it could be traced back to me, Mom. I refuse to lie in wait any longer."

"Abel, see reason—"

"I don't think I'm the one that needs to see reason," Abel snapped.

Sarah sighed. She knew her son was right. "It was very well written," she said after a moment of silence.

Abel nodded in response. He had finished eating already and didn't really feel like talking. Sarah let out another woebegone sigh and stood to leave. "I'll be back in the morning," she informed. Abel nodded once more and his mother departed.

Abel retreated back to his bedroom and took another book and then settled into an inglenook in the living room area. His eyes felt tired and all the words blurred together. Abel tried again and again to continue reading after rubbing his eyes vigorously, but his mind wouldn't allow him to focus and he found himself rereading the same paragraph over and over again, yet absorbing none of it.

Finally, he just decided to take a quick shower and get into bed. Normally he could sneak in an hour or two of sleep before the nightmares began. He curled up into a little ball and let his heavy eyelids slip shut.

CHAPTER 28

When they say *The Early Morning Chronicle*, they really aren't kidding. The next day Lucy and Keturah had woken Abel up at nearly the crack of dawn to show him *The Early Morning Chronicle* on Lucy's HoloNet. Abel skipped past the article since he knew it by heart and went on to read some of the comments. Most were indecisive, but some were negative and even fewer were positive. Abel's heart sank, but he had thought this might happen. Thus the reason he planned on writing multiple articles until he had gained supporters.

"This is pretty good actually," Keturah said. "As you can see, most of the readers don't know what to think which means they can be persuaded into agreement with the proper articles."

Abel nodded his head, scanning over the comments again. Keturah was right. Most didn't know whether they were on board with Abel or not. Looking at the other headlines, Abel's eyes were drawn to something about the Red Dragon.

He pulled it up and began to read aloud, "The recent disappearance of activity from the Red Dragon has caused quite the stir. Many theories have been tossed around, but we've gone to the source to get the truth. An anonymous government spokeswoman has announced the capture and detainment of the infamous cyberterrorist."

He didn't want to read anymore. "Those liars," he spat.

Keturah gave a noncommittal grunt and sighed. "Of course they're going to claim they did it, Abel. It makes them look good."

Abel shook his head, knowing she was right. "I have another article for tomorrow's paper," he informed Lucy. "Let me just go grab it."

Abel left the circular room, ran past the living room, and darted into his bedroom, grabbing the paper he had torn out of his notebook.

More Facts on Males and Females

That You Probably Didn't Know

By: Anonymous Submitter

So many of you probably read the article I wrote in yesterday's paper. Seeing as I am writing this before the actual article is printed, I don't know how you reacted yet, but I can mostly guess that it wasn't as positive as I would have hoped. That's okay.

So maybe today I should clear the air about males. Males are not all psychopathic. Surprise! Most males (as far as I know) are a lot like women. We are usually taller and stronger, yes. And women tend to be more emotionally attuned, but men have emotions too. (Trust me, I know.) Men are this way because they were traditionally the protectors and providers and women were traditionally the nurturers and caretakers.

So things I know about males:
We like to eat.... A lot
We like to sleep a lot too
Men like quiet (especially when trying to focus)

We hate being interrupted (especially when working)

We tend to be strategical when faced with a problem

Men's memories (unlike women's) are linked not to emotion, but to relevance to the situation at hand

We tend to be very literal; we say what we mean and mean what we say and usually have no hidden meaning

We like to eat

So there you go. Now moving on to the lies of Femater.

Femater has told you several things (or maybe not disclosed things) to you that are not true. The biggest lie being that Femater is a utopia. It isn't! There are so many things wrong with it. Most people are broke; those who aren't at work for, you guessed it, the government. The government is lying to you about issues such as poverty, overpopulation, economy, advancements, and, well, pretty much everything.

The new healthcare act? A law in disguise making it legal to kill anyone over sixty. And they're already killing babies! If that's not enough right there, they also have rewritten most of history so that it supports their agenda. I can only imagine what else they're lying about! Think about it: what's your job right now?

If you answered something other than a government position, where are you living right now? I bet it isn't in the nice neighborhoods with identical houses, perfect gardens, wonderful security systems, and high-tech appliances.

If you did answer in some government position, why are you so better off than everyone else? How are you more important than the people who grow (or in some cases manufacture) your food? The people who create all these wonderful, high-tech systems? Answer: you aren't. So why do you live in the beautiful house that's in prim condition and everyone else lives in the slums?

I want you to just think on all of this. And maybe you'll see where I'm coming from.

Abel walked back to the meeting hall and handed the paper to Lucy. She smiled at him and left through the long hallway that led to the stairs. Abel sighed and turned to Keturah.

"Your mother will be here with your breakfast soon," she informed.

Abel nodded. "I need to talk to her about Hillary."

Keturah frowned slightly. "I don't trust her. Remember, Abel: a leopard doesn't change its spots."

Abel nodded again and Keturah left just as Abel's mother walked down the hallway. She smiled at Abel and handed him his breakfast. "I saw Hillary at the meeting yesterday. What the hell was she doing here?" Abel demanded.

"Abel! Language!" his mother scolded.

Abel just raised an eyebrow at his mother and she sighed. "She wants to become a part of the revolutionary movement."

"So before she wants to kill me, but now she's my best friend?"

"Abel, see through her eyes. Her sister is dead and she blames herself. What caused her sister's death? Not supporting Harley or men. She can't live knowing that, so she changed. It made her reanalyze her choices."

Abel narrowed his eyes and let out a low snort. "Whatever."

Abel's mother gave her son a pleading look and then narrowed her own eyes. "I know you're having a hard time right now, and I've tried to be very understanding about that, but your behavior of late has been unacceptable. This brooding, rude, quiet

Abel is not one that I like. Yes, Harley did die and yes, it is tragic, but you have no excuse to take it out on those around you. I'm sick and tired of you thinking that just because she died you get to walk all over everyone around you. I just hope you realize that the more you push people away, the less they'll want to be around you and the more they'll stop trying to help until eventually you'll have nobody."

Abel felt like he had been slapped in the face...in a good way? It was like a splash of reality. He had been acting rudely towards everyone around him without even realizing it. He looked down at his feet shamefully, feeling chastened.

"I'm sorry, Mom."

Sarah didn't respond; instead, she wrapped her arms around Abel and gave a big squeeze. "You're such an amazing boy, Abel. I know this is hard right now, but it'll get better; it always does."

"You can only get rainbows after the rain," Abel whispered to himself mostly. His knees felt week, so he collapsed in the nearest chair, letting the tears that had been waiting patiently behind his eyes fall freely.

Soon he was sobbing. Sobbing and rocking back and forth with his head in his hands. He was so angry and sad and lost. Abel's mother sat next to him and rubbed his back. "Just get it all out," she whispered soothingly. "Emotions are toxic to hold inside," she cooed.

When all of Abel's tears had been cried, he sat on the ground with his eyes closed. He felt tired and emotionally drained. Sarah was still rubbing his back and occasionally whispering things like, "You can't bottle it all up," or, "There you go, sweetheart, there you go".

Abel ran a hand through his hair and looked over at his mother. "Why does it hurt so much? I thought love was supposed to be happy and beautiful."

Sarah pulled her son's head into her chest and kissed his forehead. "Ah, nothing can be happy all the time. You know it's real when it hurts. I don't pretend to know anything about love; I've never actually been in it. But I love you. It isn't necessarily the same thing, but it's the closest thing I have. You've suffered a great loss and you are so strong, Abel."

"I don't want to be strong anymore. I wish I had never left the basement that day."

"Do you? Do you really? Isn't it better to have loved, to have explored even for a short while than to be caged forever?"

"You're the one who caged me!"

"What I did, I did for love. It wasn't the smartest or the best idea, but I just wanted you to be safe. It may have been one of the most painful things; watching you grow up in solitude and in wonder about the world. 'When can I go outside, Mommy?' But I did it out of love. You don't have the luxury of being a leader and a whiner at the same time though."

For once everything was clear to Abel. Everything made sense and he understood. He wrapped his arms around his mother. "I love you," he whispered.

It's funny how often those words are said and yet how little they are meant. It's become blasé, meaningless, habitual even. They are supposed to be the most meaningful, emotional three words. They're said too much, but not meant enough.

Abel's mom smiled with tears in her eyes. "I love you, too, Abel."

And Abel could tell that she meant it. It wasn't just her responding in the customary, expected way. She loved him unconditionally with all her heart. It was a special thing, really. Something that some only dream about. Love was weird, a different meaning for each person and yet always constant and the same.

Love was beautiful and painful and strange and unintentional and purposeful all at the same time.

CHAPTER 29

The next day, Abel was surprised by a visit from Hillary. He had so many mixed emotions that he didn't know what to feel when he saw her, but surprise pretty much summed it up. She seemed embarrassed and maybe even ashamed. Abel watched her cross the meeting room carefully until she was right next to him.

She stared at the ground and cleared her throat, shifting her weight from one foot to another. "I read your articles in the paper," she said finally.

Abel swallowed the lump that was in his throat. "Is that all you came here to say?"

She met his eyes and glared at him and in that moment, she looked so much like Harley it hurt. "No. I also came to give you this."

She handed Abel on thick manila envelope. "If anyone asks, you didn't get that from me," she whispered.

Abel started to open it and Hillary slapped his hand away. "Not now, idiot."

Yup, she was definitely related to Harley.

Abel shrugged his shoulders and set the envelope next to him. "Is that all?" asked Abel.

Hillary took a deep breath and let it out slowly. "I also wanted to say that I'm sorry. I didn't know any better, but the moment I saw you holding Harley and crying, I knew. You couldn't be a vicious monster if you were that emotional about her...her passing."

Abel closed his eyes and when he reopened them Hillary was crying. "I know you...blame yourself," Abel choked out. This was the hardest thing he had ever had to say. "But you can't. You can't blame yourself for what Harley chose to do. How were you supposed to know that she was going to...take the bullet for me?" It physically pained him to say it. But he also knew that he was right. It *wasn't* Hillary's fault. He couldn't be spiteful towards her just because he was hurting; she was hurting too.

Hillary nodded and sniffled. "Thank you, Abel. Your forgiveness is so important to me because I know how important it would be to Harley."

Abel knew he had made the right decision. Hillary stood to leave. She hesitated and turned back to face Abel. Sticking out her hand, Abel shook it, but it only reminded him of Harley, making his chest constrict. "I'm glad you're giving me a chance. It means a lot to me."

Abel nodded, looking into her eyes. They were filled with pain and regret...and something else. Something that Abel couldn't quite place. It made him feel uneasy despite her obvious remorse.

He was probably just having residual anger towards her.

"Goodbye, Abel."

"See you, Har—Hillary."

Hillary gave him another sad smile and left him alone in the deafeningly silent meeting hall.

CHAPTER 30

When Abel woke up the next morning, he felt renewed. He knew that today was the day. He felt it inside of himself like a premonition. He had to step forward today.

His plan was locked and loaded. He waited patiently for his mother to arrive with his breakfast. Sarah came sauntering down the hallway at about eight. Abel met her with a hug and accepted his breakfast like always. He began to eat and his mother began to talk.

"I heard that Hillary dropped in yesterday," Abel's mom prompted.

Abel glanced over at her. "Where'd you hear that?"

"Keturah."

"Where did Keturah hear about that?"

Abel's mother laughed. "Where does Keturah hear about anything?"

"True," Abel conceded.

"So what did Hillary say?"

"Nothing much," Abel told his mom. "She apologized; I told her I forgave her." For some unknown reason, Abel didn't tell his mom about the package that Hillary had given him. He hadn't even opened it yet, but he didn't really want to open it yet.

"You told her that you forgave her?"

Abel nodded and his mom smiled. "I have something I want to do today...."

His mother frowned. "You know it's too risky to leave right now. The consequences—"

"Consequences, be damned! I don't care anymore, Mom. I'm doing this with or without your help."

Sarah sighed and shook her head. "Fine. What is it?"

Abel grinned. "I want to scope out the capitol building, firstly."

"Abel, that'd be walking right into the lion's den."

"Don't care. Secondly, I want to hand out some fliers."

"Fliers?"

"Keturah helped me make some e-fliers that erase after they've been read; untraceable, unreportable, and undetectable. I want to distribute them to people around town; inform them of what the government is doing and invite them to our meetings."

Abel's mom looked like she wanted to protest, but she held her tongue. Abel finished his breakfast as quickly as possible and went and grabbed the HSD, returning to his awaiting mother. "Are you going to come with me?" Abel asked her.

She sighed. "I guess I have to if you want to get into the capitol building. Besides, I could help you get out of a sticky situation if necessary."

Abel grinned at his mother and turned the HSD on, leading the way out the door. He hadn't been outside in what felt like forever and he was beginning to get claustrophobic in the underground hideout. As soon as he lifted the trapdoor, he sucked in a deep breath of the fresh air. It felt like he was breathing for the first time. A goofy grin found its way onto his face despite his effort to control it. He climbed up and offered his mother his hand, helping her up.

Abel closed his eyes and absorbed the beautiful noises of the forest, the breeze in the trees, the birds chirping, the dry leaves crunching under foot. This was one of the only pieces of untouched land on the planet.

When Abel reopened his eyes, his mother was staring at him with a funny expression on her face. "What?" asked Abel.

"It's good to see you happy," was all Sarah elaborated.

Abel didn't know how to respond, so he stayed silent and continued walking. His mom followed closely behind him. When they got to the road, Abel let his mom take over the leading part since he had no idea where he was going.

"A couple of precautions," Sarah warned, "you're going to see some pretty disturbing things, but you can't show that it bothers you; if anything, you have to act interested and intrigued. It would be a dead giveaway if you let it show that it bothered you."

Abel nodded. "Okay, not disturbed. Gotcha."

"You also can't say anything that can even remotely be related to males, male rights, or disagreement with the government."

Abel agreed to the terms and soon they were in front of a ginormous glass building. It towered over most of the city and stood out due to its fancy state, large wall, and surrounding guard towers. From the very top of the highest tower waved a large white flag with a red circle and cross mixture. The female symbol. Smog circled the air around the building and filled Abel's lungs; he repressed the urge to gag and cough.

"Right this way," Sarah said in a very professional voice.

She walked toward the giant gate and stopped at a little window. "Sarah Williams, SGI Department, accompanied by a guest."

"ID?" asked the woman behind the window. Sarah handed a small plastic card to the woman and she returned it after a few moments of inspection and typing a few things into her HoloNet.

"ID for the guest?"

"She doesn't have ID yet; it's still pending. She just moved here from Matriarium," Abel's mom lied smoothly.

The women looked like she wanted to say something else, but she shrugged and slipped something through the window. "Guest pass," she said monotonously.

Sarah gave a small smile. "Thank you."

"You are inspection number five."

Sarah nodded and there was a long beep and the gate slowly shuddered open, revealing a dingy, large room with ten different stations that were a labeled with a large, blocky number. Sarah walked straight up to the one labeled with a giant, peeling five. Four women stepped out from behind a small partition. "Sarah Williams, what is your ID number?"

"S6932EW."

One of the ladies typed something into her HoloNet and a little beeping noise issued. "Proceed," the lady said. Sarah walked forward and a different lady began to pat her down. After being pat down, they ushered her into what appeared to be a giant black box. The third lady pressed a few buttons on the box and a loud whirring noise ensued for about five minutes until a clicking noise began and then a door opened on the box and Abel's mom stepped out. The final lady pulled Abel's mother to the side and held a small device over the crook of her elbow until a little ticking sound issued and then they turned to look at Abel.

"Guest, state your name and ID."

"She doesn't have an ID yet; it's still pending," his mother repeated.

The first lady glanced back down at her HoloNet and nodded. "Guest, state your name."

Sarah's eyes flashed with warning, but Abel ignored her. "Abbey Normal."

Sarah looked like she wanted to slam her head into the brick wall that was beside her. Why had she told him about that old movie that she had from her great, great, great grandmother?

Abel grinned at her, looking extremely proud of himself. "Proceed," the first lady said as she typed a few things onto her HoloNet.

Abel walked forward just as his mother had and allowed the second lady to pat him down. The second lady pushed Abel into the black box thing and closed the door. It was pitch black inside too. Suddenly the thing roared to life. The whirring noise was ten times louder on the inside and bright lights began to flash from every direction, blinding Abel. The entire room was spinning too. Abel was dizzy and his head hurt; he just wanted to throw up.

Finally, after what seemed like hours, the door clicked open and Abel stumbled out. The fourth lady grabbed his elbow and pulled him over to the small table where she operated. She grabbed the small device that she had used on Abel's mom and held it over the crook of Abel's elbow too. There was a tick and suddenly a stinging pain shot through his arm. Abel hissed and tried to jerk his arm away.

"This is her first time," Sarah explained.

There was loud beep from the little device and Sarah's eyes widened. "Wh-what's wrong?" she asked, trying to sound casual.

"I'm not sure," the fourth lady said with a frown. "The test was inconclusive."

"You may proceed," the fourth lady said with the frown still fixed on her face.

Sarah's shoulders relaxed and she let out a sigh of relief. "Come on, Abbey."

Abel followed his mother through two sliding doors and down a long, dark hallway that let out into a courtyard with large green trees, lush lawns, and beautiful wooden benches. It contrasted so greatly to all that Abel had seen so far at the capitol building. He had been so distracted by the patio area that he hadn't noticed his mother was still walking and he jogged to catch up.

Sarah led the way through another set of sliding doors, though these weren't dingy or creaky or shuddering. This set moved smoothly and the glass was so clear that it didn't even look like it was there.

They opened to reveal a bright, white waiting room. Everything was white. White walls, white chairs, white trim, white clothes, white floors, white lights, white, white, white....

Abel's mom walked up to the white desk and smiled at the lady seated behind it. She must've been in her early twenties and had black hair that was twisted up into a neat, perfect bun. "Good morning, Agatha," Sarah greeted. "I'm giving Abbey a tour of the building. She's eighteen and she thinks she might be interested in working at the capitol building."

"Morning, Sarah. Wow, it feels like just yesterday that you were giving me my tour. Remember: no restricted areas," Agatha said with a perfect smile.

Sarah nodded and offered a tight-lipped smile of her own. "Let's go, Abbey."

Sarah led down a bright hallway with around twenty doors on each side. "This is the office area," Abel's mom informed.

She continued to the end of the hallway where a tubular glass chamber was. "Okay, you're going to go first," Mrs. Williams told her son. "I'm going to manually operate it from here. You are going to rise off the ground. Do *not* panic and do *not* move. When you get the second floor, wait for me there."

Abel nodded and his mom ushered him into the glass chamber. She began to press a few buttons on the console next to it and metal door slid shut. When Abel looked back to his feet, he was startled to see them raised off the ground by about a foot. "Woah!" Abel exclaimed as he twisted his upper body around to get a better look.

"Stop moving," his mother commanded from below. Her voice sounded muffled through the door.

Abel righted himself again and stayed still. Eventually he stopped moving upwards and the cylinder's door slid back open. "Floor 2," a robotic voice announced. Abel stepped out into a circular, white room that was completely empty.

He waited until his mother appeared next to him. "What was that?" he asked.

"An anti-gravity chamber. It allows you to move from floor to floor without using the stairs."

She gestured for Abel to follow her. "This is the Male Eradication floor. Everything here is devoted to keeping males gone."

They walked down a hallway. "To your left is the male discovery and prevention team and to the right is the MES, male eradication squad."

Abel looked to his right and saw a circular room filled with about forty people. He recognized one of them as the woman who had been sent to shoot him. A surge of rage powered through his chest and he just wanted to rip her head off.

"Let's keep moving," Abel's mom suggested, gently resting her hand on Abel's shoulder and guiding him through the hallway.

She pushed Abel a little further forward and showed him all the rooms on that floor. All of them relating to male eradication.

She took Abel up another floor, floor three, the SGI department. "This one may be disturbing," Sarah warned. "You do have to wear protective gear."

Abel was a little disconcerted at first but then it dawned on him that it was for the protection of the infants. He suited up along with his mother and they plunged into the room.

Immediately to the left, there was a large room with glass walls. Sarah led inside; it was empty. On the far wall, there were glass compartments. In the one to the very far left, there were about twenty bubble-like things floating in the center and heat radiated off of it. Inside each bubble were a tiny, little circular jelly-like substance and a little squiggly line, swimming around. On the surface of each bubble, were a series of numbers.

The next glass compartment over was labeled 'eight weeks' and inside were about twenty bubbles as well, except each bubble was filled with what looked like a tiny shrimp with a placenta that was attached to a tube from the top of the bubble. In the next compartment, labeled 'twelve weeks', there were about fifteen bubbles and in each one, the shrimp-like thing now had little arms and legs and was a little under double the previous size. The next glass compartment had about twelve bubbles and was labeled 'sixteen weeks'. Inside each bubble was what resembled a tiny baby about the size of an avocado.

Abel's stomach began to turn. He thought he understood why this room would be disturbing now.

The next compartment to the right had about ten bubbles and was labeled 'twenty weeks'. Each bubble had a fetus that was about the length of a banana. You could easily tell now that it was a human baby. Abel's heart was pounding. The next compartment, labeled 'twenty-four weeks', had about eight bubbles, each with a fetus the length of about a foot. It was more proportionally developed now. Abel rushed to the next compartment. Six bubbles. 'Twenty-eight weeks'. The bubble's fetuses now had eyes that could open and close, eyelashes, and it was starting to plump up. It was probably about two inches longer too.

Abel hurried to the next one. 'Thirty-two weeks'. Four bubbles. The fetuses now had nails and hair and had gotten considerably plumper and about two more inches longer. 'Thirty-six weeks'. Two bubbles. Each one was about the size of a head of romaine lettuce and looked a lot plumper. 'Forty weeks'. One bubble....

Inside was a fully formed baby.

"This one's ready," Abel's mom said. She pressed a few buttons on the outside of the glass and the embryonic fluid sac popped and the baby gently lowered to the bottom of the compartment where it immediately began to cry.

Sarah opened a little door at the bottom of the glass wall and pulled the baby out. "Do you want to hold her?"

Abel couldn't help but smile at the tiny infant. Sarah laid the baby into Abel's arms and she instantly stopped crying, letting out a long yawn and wrapping her tiny hand around Abel's thumb. Abel rocked gently back and forth and the baby cooed slightly before closing her eyes and drifting off to sleep.

Sarah smiled at her son. "You're a natural."

"Mom?"

"Yes, Abel?"

"Why do the bubbles decrease each four-week period?"

He wasn't sure that he wanted to know. Sarah closed her eyes and let out a breath. "We select the best from each four-week period, slowly eradicating the rest until we only have one baby with the best genes. We get to choose and program the babies the way we want genetically and then we pick the one's that'll be most likely to be unquestioning, docile, and obedient."

Abel didn't know what to say, so he just cuddled the baby closer to his chest.

"Let's get her to the nursery," Sarah suggested.

Abel nodded and followed his mother out of the glass room and down the hallway to a room filled with cribs and crying babies. His mom told him to sit the baby down into the empty crib and he did so gently as to not wake her. Then he went around to all the cribs and comforted the crying babies until they too fell back asleep.

The rest of the tour, Abel didn't really pay attention. His mom seemed to notice his stupor because she sighed on the last floor and said. "I'm going to show you something that you aren't supposed to see on a tour."

Abel snapped his head up, his mother's words catching his attention. "What?" he asked.

"The basement."

Abel knitted his eyebrows. "What's so special about the basement?"

"You'll see," his mother assured.

They walked to the anti-gravity chamber of descent (apparently it was different from the anti-gravity chamber of ascent). He slowly descended down to the very bottom floor, the basement.

Sarah arrived a little while after Abel. The basement was dark and dingy just like the outside of the building. It was filled with cells on each side of a long hallway and each cell had...a male?

They all sat stilly on their beds with the occasional stiff movement. Each one was wearing all black and stared blankly ahead.

"The government harbors men?!"

"Yes. They use mind control to keep them in check and whatnot. They use them for the jobs that they either don't want to do or can't do."

"That's so hypocritical!"

"I know, Abel. You're preaching to the choir, babe."

Abel let out a long sigh and glared at the ground. "That's disgusting."

Sarah nodded and ushered Abel to the anti-gravity chamber of ascent. Abel floated up to the ground floor and his mom followed closely behind him. Abel knew one thing for sure: the government's secret male cache wasn't going to stay secret much longer.

CHAPTER 31

After handing out the fliers with his mom, Abel returned to the meeting hall with his new information. He knew that he had to sit down and write another article before he forgot anything that he had seen.

Abel hurried back to his bedroom and grabbed his notebook and pen.

Secrets

By: Anonymous Submitter

Previous articles that I've written expressed that the government is lying to you, but I didn't go into much depth. Well, I can now inform you of the magnitude of their lies that they've told. The government has a secret cache of males. Yes, I repeat, a secret, underground supply of men. I've seen it myself.

You know why they have it? They keep a few males for the jobs they either CANT do or won't do. Things that they either find beneath themselves or things that they literally are not capable of accomplishing.

Did you know that they also dispose of 90% of SGI babies? 90%! That's crazy. So not only are they pretending that your children are sick just to kill them, but nine tenths of all babies don't even make it to week forty of incubation.

Do they feel any remorse with all these lies and murders? Nope. They don't care because they have money and power and *everything about their lives is perfect. They don't care about the millions of other lives that are complete crap because, hey, theirs is fine!*

Remember that next time you turn to the government for help or solutions: they don't care!

Abel was fairly satisfied with it, so he closed the notebook and set it aside. He grabbed a book that his mother had packed for him and settled in next to the fireplace, reading and rereading until he had practically memorized the entire book.

He couldn't get that sweet little baby out of his head. Deciding that he needed to relax, Abel went to take a nice, long shower and then collapsed into bed, wanting nothing more than a long, restful sleep that he hadn't had in a very long time.

Restful? No. Dreamless? No. Annoying? You bet.

Abel dreamed of Harley again. Her lifeless body in his arm and the deafening boom of the gun. He couldn't get the image out of his head. When he jerked awake, his whole body was shaking and covered in sweat. His breathing was ragged and his heart was pounding in his throat. He wondered what time it was.

He padded out to the meeting hall and glanced at the clock. 2:15. He knew that there was no way that he was going back to sleep, so he settled into the chair by the fire and picked up his book. He must have accidentally fallen asleep while reading because when he reopened his eyes, his book had slid to the floor, his neck had a horrible crick, and his mother was standing in front of him with breakfast.

"Morning, sweetie," she greeted upon seeing Abel open his eyes.

"Morning, Mom. What time is it?" Abel asked groggily as he rubbed his eyes.

"It's a little after seven."

Abel accepted his breakfast and handed his mother the article he had written. "When you get a chance, will you please give this to Lucy?"

Sarah eyed the ripped-out notebook paper carefully. "Do you realize that right now one of the government's main priorities is finding the author of these newspaper articles?"

Abel grinned. "Good."

Sarah frowned. "How is that good, Abel?"

"If they pull the newspaper, it makes it look like they don't want it to be read. What other reason would they not want it to be read besides that it's true? If they make a public statement, it draws attention to it and makes it seem, once again, true. Whatever solution they come up with makes the article look more reliable and the government less so."

Sarah sighed. "I guess you're right."

Abel gave a triumphant smile and continued eating. He loved that he was stirring up trouble and it felt great. Was this what it felt like to be a rebel? Now he understood why Harley was so rebellious. It was exhilarating, exciting, and nerve-wracking all at once. But most at all, it felt like a sip of freedom. No, not a sip, the whole barrel of freedom. And Abel loved it.

His mom was gone within the hour, promising to take the article to Lucy. Abel was by himself. Again. He was really running out of things to do with his infinite free time. He sighed and rubbed his eyes again.

A yawn escaped his lips and he figured that trying to go back to sleep couldn't hurt. He slunk back to his bedroom and flopped onto his bed, wrapping the blanket around himself and letting the warmth envelop him.

CHAPTER 32

Lucy knew that this would probably be her last print. She had received multiple notices that if she didn't stop printing the articles that Abel was giving her then the government would shut down her facility. She felt the imminence in the statement and that's what pressed her to do an early publishing of the paper; as soon as Sarah had given her the article, Lucy had set to work and the paper was ready to be uploaded at around 5:00 p.m.

About ten minutes after she had published the article, there was a banging on the door. Lucy was tentative to open it and in the few seconds that she had hesitated, the door burst open and fell off its hinges. Lucy let out a small squeal and jumped back into the corner of the room. Twenty burly people dressed in all black and wearing masks, helmets, and body armor slammed into the small publishing studio and began throwing things around, breaking everything, stomping, and shattering.

Lucy watched in horror as her life's work was demolished right before her eyes. One of the large, ominous people reared back their arm to throw something onto the ground and the flash of silver caught Lucy's eye. Her mother's locket. She couldn't let him destroy it.

She didn't even realize what she was doing, but she grabbed the person's arm and they slowly turned to face her. "Let go," they growled. Their voice was much deeper than Lucy had expected, but she didn't release.

"Th-this is pr-private property," Lucy squeaked.

The person jerked their arm away and slammed Lucy into the wall causing her vision to blur. She closed her eyes and tried to soothe the pounding pain in her head and throbbing in her spine. The person smashed the locket right in front of Lucy and then grabbed her by her hair, yanking her up and slamming her against the wall again.

"You have impeded our mission," the deep robotic voice snarled. "You must be destroyed."

Lucy couldn't think straight with the pain roaring through her head and the warm trickle down the back of her neck, but she didn't like the sound of 'being destroyed'. The person dropped her to the ground and Lucy curled up into a fetal position, not being able to think or do anything else.

Her vision was so blurry that she couldn't see and her few movements were sluggish and listless. Smoke filled Lucy's nostrils and the heat was unbearable, but Lucy couldn't move. Noise roared in her ears, encouraging the pounding headache. So hot. Finally her vision blacked out and she lost all feeling everywhere. She closed her eyes and let the hot noise consume her.

CHAPTER 33

When Abel woke up, his mom and Keturah were waiting in the meeting hall. They both stood upon seeing him.

"Abel," his mother breathed. "Oh, Abel."

Abel frowned. "What's wrong?"

"They certainly shut down her operation," Keturah barked. She held up her HoloNet and it displayed a moving picture of flames roaring around a small building. Abel could just make out the words 'The Early Morning Chronicle' displayed across the roof.

The longer Abel stared at the picture, the more dread built up in his chest. "Wait, can you zoom in on the door?"

Keturah knitted her eyebrows, but she nodded and fidgeted with the HoloNet for a moment, turning it back around to show Abel the finished product.

Just before the whole building erupted in flames, there was a flash of black across the screen, almost imperceptible. "Slow it down," Abel commanded.

Keturah did and turned it back to Abel. There was a flash of twenty people in all black exiting the building. Someone had sloppily tried to edit the picture and missed some.

He pointed it out to his mom and Keturah. "Oh my gosh!" his mother gasped, slapping her hand to her mouth.

"Wouldn't you say that those people are way too large to be women?" Abel suggested.

Keturah nodded solemnly. "A little ironic considering what your last article was about."

"Was—was Lucy in the building?" Abel finally built up the courage to ask.

Keturah gave another mournful nod. Abel turned and ran his hands through his hair. How many people had to die for this cause?

Abel shook his head and turned back to face his mother who had her hand clamped to her mouth and tears streaming down her face. What time was it?

He glanced at the clock and it read just a little past seven. Had he really slept for that long?

"Did she publish the article?" Abel asked.

Keturah nodded. "I think that's what spurred this attack."

Abel sighed and ran his hand through his hair again. "What was the reaction earned from the article *and* the fire?"

"You should see the uproar," Keturah said with a smirk. "At least something good came from it."

Abel grinned and even caught a hint of a smile on his mother's face. He had caused that. He had prompted the rioting. And it felt amazing. It felt amazing to be a part of something bigger than himself, something bigger than everything he'd known so far in his eighteen years. Rebellion felt amazing.

Abel sat down in one of the chairs and shook his head in awe and sadness and admiration. He had done that. He had....

Wow.

"So what now?" asked Abel. "Now we wait, we let the tension build, we recruit, and eventually, when we're bigger than the government and completely prepared, we attack. They stand no chance."

Abel grinned like a fool. Keturah sounded so sure that it made Abel feel reassured in this plan, it made Abel feel like he could do anything as long as he stood behind her. All of this was so empowering.

"Now we wait," Abel's mom echoed.

Now we wait, Abel thought. *Story of my life.*

CHAPTER 34

Abel knew all about waiting. And he hated it. He hated waiting when he could easily be doing so much. It made him feel powerless. Abel hated feeling powerless.

A week creeped by and Abel heard news from his mother about all the riots, protests, strikes, chaos, the government's helplessness. Abel figured that if he had to wait at least he could wait with the knowledge that not everyone else was waiting too.

Downside of waiting: thinking. When Abel let his mind wander, it always wound up at the same spot: Harley. He had never known that it was possible to be in so much pain and still be alive. But time moved on, marching on without a doubt and Abel was still alive....

The what-ifs ate him alive. What if Harley hadn't taken the bullet? What if the shot hadn't killed her? What if the situation was reversed? Would he take the bullet for her? His answer was immediate: yes. A thousand times over. Every. Single. Time.

Abel knew it was pointless to think these things and that he was just torturing himself, but how do you stop thinking? How do you turn off your brain?

He felt a migraine forming at the base of his skull, pounding through his eye. He had had too little sleep and too much stress and it was beginning to show. Abel was beginning to look ragged and tattered with stubble sprouting from his chin and unkempt hair sticking out in every direction, and he was beginning to feel frayed and at wits end. His nerves were shot and his blood-shot eyes conveyed only a tenth of the tiredness that Abel felt.

He really couldn't think of anything to do; he couldn't write anymore newspaper articles, he had read every book at least ten times, sleeping was out of the question, and he had already taken the longest shower in the entire history of showers. Time to get inventive.

Abel stood from the edge of his bed and walked across the room, into the living area, and into the bathroom. There were tons of cabinets in here and Abel had yet to explore them all. He figured that most, if not all, of them contained bathroom supplies. But what else did he have to do?

The first few cabinets were filled with the expected: towels, toilet paper, toothpaste, shampoo, conditioner, and the like. But when Abel reached the fifth one over on the bottom, he was surprised. After shifting a jumbo pack of toothbrushes, he revealed a leather-bound notebook. Abel pursed his lips and opened the cover. On the inside, a name was written: Harley Haim.

Property of Harley Haim

Abel slammed the book shut and slowly reopened it. Why did Harley have a notebook stashed in the bathroom of a secret, underground bunker? He flipped it to the first page.

So I guess I need something to do while hiding out in Keturah's little barracks. Thank everything good in the world that she allows me to stay here when Hillary gets unbearable. Today Hillary was on my ass about the importance of school and harping about how I shouldn't skip and that I should get an internship so I can get a good job and she just wouldn't stop yelling. God, she makes me crazy.

So I guess that this is kind of like a journal. I hate the word diary, so no way will it ever be referred to as that.

I ran into Keturah when I was skipping one day. She and her revolutionists are what've kept me sane as of late. It makes me feel like I'm doing something, like I'm needed. Whenever I don't feel like going home, Keturah lets me stay here. So often. It's funny how little we all appreciate what we have. We take EVERYTHING for granted.

Just today, I passed this little girl and her mother at the store and the little girl was complaining about how she wanted a brand new HoloCom. She must've been six! Why does she even need a HoloCom? And why isn't she grateful that she has one at all? Most ADULTS don't have HoloComs.

Harley Haim

That was the end of the first entry. Abel slowly flipped through the book to the very back. The last entry. The entire page was smudged as though Harley had been crying when she wrote it and her scrawl was messier like her hand was shaking.

I'm going to do it....

There isn't a point anyways. What role do I have on this planet? None. I have no purpose and I HATE my life. What do I have to look forward to? Nothing is ever going to change. Ever. So to anyone reading this (which I doubt there are), goodbye.

Goodbye....

For good.

Abel checked the date at the top of the page. The day before he had bumped into Harley. The day before she was planning kill herself. She hadn't written another entry after she met Abel.

He couldn't believe that he was the one to stumble across it. Crazy coincidence? Serendipity? Who knew? Abel sure didn't, but it made his heart pound to think about.

Abel closed the book gently and hugged it to his chest. It was all he had left of Harley. He exited the bathroom and sat in his chair next to the fire. Harley had probably sat there. Harley had lived where he was living. Abel sat the book down and walked into the bedroom. All the beds looked the same except the one Abel had claimed; its sheets were strewn all across the bed and floor and the blanket had been removed from Abel waking up sweating. He inspected each bed a little closer and found that one had no dust on any of the bedposts while the others had accumulated a light coating over the course of not being used for who knew how long.

The bunk right above his.

Harley would be the person that wanted the top bunk. It was perfectly made and completely neat. Abel flopped onto his own, messy bed and frowned when he heard a crinkling beneath him. He sat up and flung his legs off the bed revealing the manila envelope that Hillary had given him. He had completely forgotten about it.

Abel carefully opened and slid the contents out onto his bed. It was a giant, folded map. Abel unfolded it and inspected it. It was a map of the capitol building, highlighting weak points, known entry points and escapes, vital security rooms, and vital structural support. Hillary was trying to help them invade the capitol? Under one entrance in particular Hillary had written: best option.

Abel studied the map carefully and slowly a grin spread across his face; Keturah was going to love this.

CHAPTER 35

He had been right. Keturah was enthralled when he showed her the highly detailed map. His mom gave him an I-told-you-so look, obviously thinking that this proved that Hillary had changed, and Abel agreed.

"This is perfect!" Keturah exclaimed. "I have scouts that have been mapping the place out, but I thought it would take us years to get this much detail. This is absolutely perfect!"

Abel couldn't help but grin satisfactorily. "Perfect," Keturah muttered under her breath while inspecting the layout closer.

"We had better go," Abel's mother reminded Keturah.

"Right. Later, kiddo."

"Do you have to leave? It's so quiet when I'm by myself; it drives me insane."

Keturah smiled. "I'm afraid so, but I think I have a solution." She walked over to the far wall in the meeting room and opened a cabinet that Abel had also never noticed; for someone who spent all day every day in the same room, he was very unobservant of his surroundings.

Behind the cabinet was a HoloMuse.The cool thing about HoloMuses is that they analyzed the music and provided a visual representation of the analysis of the song.

Sarah's forehead was slightly creased with worry. "Do you really think that's a good idea? What if someone hears?"

"It's fine," Keturah scoffed. "No one will be able to hear this entire facility is soundproofed." She turned back to Abel. "Just mess around with it a little bit; you'll get the hang of it. Have fun!"

She gesticulated for Sarah to follow her out and the two women left, leaving Abel staring device.

Abel filtered through the flat, small squares with glowing blue writing on them until he found one that looked promising. He popped it in and an unknown sound filled the speakers. He really liked it. It definitely filled the silence that killed him. There was some sort of pounding, and something that sounded deep and thumping, and something that took up most of the sound that was fluid and driven, there was someone singing, and so many other sounds that blended together to make one cohesive noise.

Deciding to do something productive with his weekend, Abel began to set up for Monday's meeting, pulling chairs around, tidying up, and writing down the topics. He couldn't gather the papers or anything like that because only Keturah knew how to access that.

After he had finished, he pulled over the secure HoloNet that Keturah had in the meeting hall. He opened up the news headlines and immediately one caught his attention: The Return of the Red Dragon. But Harley was dead. There was no way. Unless...

Abel's thoughts were interrupted when he heard something behind him and turned expecting to see his mother or Keturah. What he did not expect to see were around twenty burly figures dressed in all back, wearing helmets and armor. The people who had burned down Lucy's place.

"Can I help you?" asked Abel in almost a threatening tone.

There was no response.

The people, Abel was sure they were men, began throwing around chairs, crushing everything in their paths.

"Hey!" Abel exclaimed

They didn't stop. Abel wasn't sure what to do. He grabbed the one nearest to him, a person who was a little shorter and scrawnier than him, and restrained them. Everyone stopped and turned to look at Abel.

"You have impeded our mission," they all said in the same robotic, monotonous voice. "You must be destroyed."

Abel didn't want to be destroyed. All of the others surged towards him and Abel, in a panic, let go of the one he was holding. The first one to approach Abel threw a punch that Abel swiftly avoiding and returned instinctually. He didn't know where this was coming from, but he grabbed the next one by the neck and pulled it down, jerking his knee into the person's stomach. When he turned to see who was coming next, a fist slammed into his jaw, making his vision blur slightly and throwing him back into the wall. Abel stood and assessed the next person coming at him. He knew that he couldn't win, but he wasn't going down without a fight.

He charged at the closest person and rammed them in the stomach, tackling them in the process. Someone grabbed his shoulder from behind and threw him back into the wall, hitting the HoloMuse in the process and it emitted a high-pitched squealing noise. All of the people clapped their hands to their ears and fell to their knees, moaning. When the noise stopped, Abel watched as the men shuddered, relaxed, and then shook their head, standing back up.

Abel readied himself for another barrage of attacks, but the men stood where they were. When Abel saw that an attack wasn't coming, the adrenaline that had been pumping through his veins began to wear off and his head felt light and he felt dizzy. Pain throbbed up his jaw, through the back of his skull, and pounded down his neck.

One of the men turned to another and said, "Dude, what—how—?"

"Justin?" the guy who had been turned to said quizzically. "How are we in control?"

"Wait, wait, wait, back up," Abel said. Everyone turned to face him and they all looked mildly surprised. "Can you guys take off your helmets and stuff? It's hard to talk to you like that."

"We need to get out of this armor," one of the men shouted. "They've probably already noticed we've gone offline and we don't want them to be able to track us."

There were murmurs of agreement and the men started stripping until they were just wearing a black t-shirt and black cargo pants. Then the one who had spoken before gathered all the armor and jogged it outside of the bunker, returning a few minutes later.

"Who *are* you?" Abel asked.

The first guy—Abel thought his name was Justin—stepped forward. "We are the men that the government has mind controlled to do whatever they want. I'm Justin and this is Garrett," he said gesturing to the person he had originally spoken to. "We were raised in captivity; I guess you could say. When I was twelve, they had developed the BWS, brain wave simulator, and we were all implanted. We haven't been in control of ourselves since; everything that we did was like we were looking in on ourselves doing it. We couldn't control it orstop it. We weren't even really aware of it."

"So why did it stop now?" wondered Garrett.

Abel snapped his fingers. "The HoloMuse! When I hit it, a high-pitched noise sounded. It must have disabled the BWS's!"

There were murmurs of agreement throughout the twenty-ish men.

"So, uh, I'm Abel," Abel introduced. "Eighteen, last male, or so I thought, uh, leader of the rebellion."

"We know," they all chorused.

"Well, not the specifics," Justin clarified, "but we know you're the last male and the leader of the rebellion. I'm Justin. Nineteen, previously a slave."

"Garrett," Garrett introduced, holding out his hand. "Nice right hook," he added with a smirk as he shook Abel's hand, gesturing to the bruise blooming across his face.

"Peter," the smaller one that Abel had been restraining said. "Sixteen."

The next one stepped forward; Abel was pretty sure that he was the one that he had tackled. "I'm William, eighteen. You have a hard head, dude."

William pushed one of the younger ones forward. "This is Gabriel. He doesn't talk much. He's fourteen."

Another of the older boys stepped up next to Gabriel and rested a hand on his shoulder. "I'm Quincy and I'm sixteen; you could say that all three of us, Gabe, Will, and I, are brothers. Our eggs came from the same donor."

Quincy grinned and motioned for the next boy to speak. "Isaiah," was all he said.

The next one stepped forward and grinned, wiping his mop of blond hair out of his eyes. "I'm Lee. Oldest here at all of twenty and yet, somehow, Justin always ends up in charge."

"That would be because you have the maturity of a five-year-old," Justin scoffed.

Lee shrugged and grinned again. "Sorry 'bout your face. It's kind of...swollen," he finally decided, though it sounded as though that wasn't the word he had wanted to say.

"'I'm Matthew," the next person said. He had a slight accent that Abel couldn't quite place. "Seventeen."

"Austin," the next one said. "'I'm eighteen and I am hungry. The regimen they had us on was so crappy. Three meals a day of this liquefied sludge that was supposedly the perfect balance of nutrients to keep us healthy on top of our daily exercises. The only variable they forgot was *taste*."

Then final one stepped forward. "Jesse. I'm sixteen and supposedly related to Austin, but I really don't see the resemblance. He's so annoying and stupid and ugly and...*annoying*."

Austin slung an arm over Jesse's shoulder and grinned toothily. "You know you love me."

Jesse rolled his eyes, but smiled nonetheless.

Apparently there weren't as many as Abel had originally thought. He did a quick count: eleven. Close enough.

"So what now?" Justin asked.

"Now it's my turn for introductions," Abel said. And so he told them everything. Raised in the basement, snuck out, caught by Harley (talking about her was so painful), the events leading up to her death, her death, the events since, his growing knowledge, the growing rebellion. Everything.

They listened in silence and when he was done, Austin whistled appreciatively. "Wow. I thought we had it bad."

Abel scratched the back of his neck. "It's not that—you guys—my life isn't that bad," he muttered.

Lee grinned. "And modest. I like you, Abe. I vote Justin out! All hail King Abel!"

Justin smacked him and rolled his eyes. "Ignore everything that he says," he advised to Abel.

"Hey!" Lee protested.

"So *now* what?" asked Garrett.

Abel glanced at the clock. "My mom should be here soon." It was surprising how much time had passed.

"Your mom?" William queried. "What does she have to do with this?"

"Well, normally Keturah comes with her," Abel told them. "And she brings food," he added as an afterthought.

Austin threw his hand into the air. "I vote we wait for Mom-Lady!"

"Shut up," Jesse said, shoving his brother.

Abel was starting to understand the dynamics of these guys a little bit. Justin was the leader and Garrett was his right-hand man. William, Gabriel, and Quincy, the three brothers, stood together and Quincy seemed pretty easy-going. William was also pretty laid-back and Abel couldn't get a read on Gabriel.

Austin and Lee were goofballs but Jesse and Justin kept them in check. He didn't really know Isaiah or Matthew that well, but Peter just seemed shy.

"Let me give you the grand tour," Abel jested. "So this is the meeting room and you guys just destroyed it. Yay!"

"Sorry, Abel," Lee said, scratching the back of his neck.

"It's not your fault. Besides, you're going to help me to clean it up."

Justin grinned. "Seems fair."

"Right this way," Abel said, leading the boys into the living room. "This is the living room where you, you know, live. There's a fireplace and couches and such. To your left is the bedroom filled with bunks and to the right is the bathroom."

"Can I have top bunk?" Austin asked Jesse.

Jesse rolled his eyes. "You can have whatever bunk you get."

Austin pouted and crossed his arms with a huff. Abel led into the bedroom and the boys quickly paired off picking beds. Justin and Garrett, William and

Gabriel, Quincy and Isaiah, Matthew and Lee, Austin and Jesse, Peter and....

He stood alone in the middle of the room and Abel's heart went out to the poor fellow. "Why don't you bunk with me, Peter?"

Peter glanced over at Abel with one hand gripping his elbow on his other arm. A ghost of a smile appeared on his face and he nodded with his ears turning a light pink. He walked over to join Abel; all the other boys were chatting and not really paying attention.

"I hope you wanted top bunk," Abel said with a grin.

Peter looked up from where he had previously been staring, the ground. The ghost of a smile grew into a close-mouthed simper. "Thank you," he said in a low voice with his ears tinging red again.

"No problem, buddy, I've been where you are." Abel clapped him on the shoulder.

Peter looked taken aback, but he didn't say anything. Abel gave a knowing smile. "I was pretty awkward when I first got out. Heck, I'm still pretty awkward."

Peter shook his head disbelievingly. "I bet you were never shy like me," Peter whispered.

"You want to hear a secret?"

Peter pursed his lips and nodded.

"I told you about Harley, right?" Peter nodded again. "Well, she was my secret weapon. She managed to bring the best out of everyone. She taught me to be myself and own it. Without her I'd probably still be as awkward as a baby giraffe. Never be afraid to be yourself. No matter what, okay? Never compromise yourself for someone else."

"Abel?" he heard his mother question from the meeting hall. "Abel, are you okay? Abel!" Her voice escalated in panic as she spoke.

"I'm fine, Mom!" Abel called, catching the other boys' attention.

"Why are the chairs scattered everywhere?" she asked as she walked through the threshold of the bedroom. "My word!" she exclaimed, dropping the bag of food that she had been holding.

"What's wrong?" Keturah asked as she appeared beside Abel's mother. "Oh my goodness!"

"Well, there goes the food," Austin complained.

Jesse socked him in the arm and muttered something that sounded suspiciously like "shut up".

"Abel, wh-what is going on?!" his mother exclaimed.

"Uh, meet my new friends, Mom. They were, uh, sent to kill me."

"Abel, you had better be joking."

"Well, technically speaking, Mrs. Williams, we were not sent to kill Abel; we were sent to get Keturah's plans and whatnot, but Abel tried to stop us, so...then came the destroying," Justin interjected.

"Abel, explain. Now," Sarah snapped in her most authoritative voice.

"These are the mind-controlled boys that you showed me. They came to, well, destroy, and when I fought back, I got slammed into the stereo and the high-pitched noise it made broke the device in their brains."

"*Slammed*?!" Sarah cried out.

"Mom, it's no big deal."

"Let me see," she cooed.

Abel sighed and trudged over to where she was standing, letting her examine his face and neck. "Oh goodness, Abel," she breathed.

"It's not *that* bad is it?"

Lee scratched the back of his neck. "It's pretty bad."

"I need to sit down," Sarah murmured.

She crumpled onto the bed that Lee was standing next to. "I didn't do it!" he exclaimed, holding up his hands.

Keturah, who had been silent the entire time, raised her eyebrows. "So now there are twelve of you?"

"Um, yes?" Abel responded.

Keturah nodded and walked back out to the meeting hall. Abel followed with the other boys trailing close behind him.

"Is this all the boys that the government had?" Keturah asked.

Justin was the one who answered. "This is all that's left of us. They had to terminate all the others."

Abel didn't ask how many they had started with.

Keturah nodded and picked up one of the knocked over chairs, sitting on it. "So most of you got BWS implants at less than twelve. How do you all know each other so well?" asked Abel.

"Each day we got one hour where we were free to talk amongst ourselves. They found that people who were under mind control 24/7 had...adverse reactions," Justin informed.

Abel grimaced. Their whole situation was just horrible. It made Abel sick. Everything that this society was trying to get away with made Abel sick.

Austin grinned despite the somber mood that had settled across the room. "During the one hour, I would always pull some sort of prank on the guards that just drove them crazy. Like one time, I switched out their lunches because of the thirty women guarding us, almost all of them had some sort of intolerance: gluten, lactose, nuts, soy, vegan, something. It was nothing that would actually hurt them, but it drove them crazy and they'd all start fighting about who had switched them out."

"That was you?" Jesse marveled.

Austin gave an evil smirk. "Yup. I may be annoying, but at least I put it to good use."

Justin shook his head and chuckled. "Sometimes I question your sanity."

Austin wiggled his eyebrows and Jesse rolled his eyes.

Abel turned his attention to William and Gabriel who seemed to be having some sort of silent conversation. Gabriel was shaking his head adamantly and William stood with his arms crossed and had one eyebrow risen. Gabriel glared at William and William narrowed his own eyes. Abel approached them, not drawing much notice from the other boys who were horsing around.

"Is there a problem, guys?" Abel asked.

Gabriel stared William down some more and William broke the eye contact. "No. Gabe's just being a stubborn brat."

Gabriel glared harder (if possible) at his brother.

"Can I be of assistance?" Abel queried.

William shrugged. "It's not a big deal. I was just trying to get Gabe to talk to you since you seem to be the guy in charge around here. He can talk; he just doesn't like to."

"Oh, well, I wouldn't say—I'm not—that's a bit of an exaggeration. I'm not a leader."

"That may be true, but you seem like a pretty cool guy and you're obviously important to whatever it is we're doing."

Abel looked at his feet, feeling his cheeks heat up slightly.

"Come one, Gabe," William urged. "Just talk to the guy."

Gabriel glared at William but said, "I barely even talk to you, so why would I converse with some stranger?"

"Whatever," Abel said with a shrug. "I'm not here to push anyone around or out of their comfort zone or whatever."

Gabe met Abel's eyes for the first time and he was silent for a moment before saying, "Thanks."

William grinned and Quincy walked over. "Hey, Abel?" Abel turned his attention to the third brother. "Lee said that your mom's awake."

Abel nodded and went to go back to the bedrooms. He was surprised to see a vast amount of the boys following him. Sarah was sitting up on Lee's bed, pressing her palm against her forehead. The boys lingered in the doorway, not getting too close.

"Hey, Mom," Abel said gently. "How are you feeling?"

She shook her head. "I had the oddest dream; there were more boys and they were living here with you and—oh my god," she whispered, catching sight of the boys in the doorway. "It wasn't a dream."

Justin took a tentative step forward. "I'm Justin," he introduced. "Oh, wow.... You're the same Sarah that would sneak us newspapers and extra food!"

Sarah's eyes widened slightly. "You remember that?"

"Sure! Before they developed the mind control technology, you would come down every Saturday and bring us stuff and tell us how things would be different one day."

Matthew grinned. Abel hadn't really heard him talk much. "You always manage to make us feel like there was hope."

Sarah let a small smile grace her face. "Well, I always thought of Abel when I talked to you guys."

Abel noticed Austin eyeing the food that had been picked up and set on one of the beds. "Mom, can you go get some more food for the boys. And supplies like clothes. You can just get some of mine; they should fit these guys for the most part and I know how hard it is to come by boy clothes. Maybe this weekend we can help you make more."

"Sure. I'll go get you all some dinner and clothes and other stuff that you might need."

Abel's mom stood and went to leave, glancing back at the boys and shaking her head slightly. Abel watched her leave and turned to the guys. "If there's anyone that wants to shower, the bathroom is right across the room."

Matthew nodded and said, "I could do with a shower."

"Yeah, you could," Garrett muttered. "We all could. Let's go, people."

"They don't have to shower if they don't want to," Matthew said, glaring at Garrett.

"Shut up, Mattie. No one asked you."

Matthew clenched his fists. "Don't call me Mattie," he seethed.

"Guys," Quincy interceded, "it's not a big deal. We can all just do what we want, okay?"

Matthew grumbled something under his breath and Garrett glared at him, looking slightly smug. Matthew stormed out of the room and into the bathroom. The other boys dispersed, leaving Abel and Quincy.

"What's their deal?" Abel asked.

"They never really got along. Matt doesn't like being bossed around and Garrett *loves* bossing people around. He's a little bigheaded and likes to have power, but he's a good guy...most of the time."

Abel pondered this, letting Quincy's words sink in. "Are there any other rivalries that I should know about?"

"Well, Isaiah and Jesse never got along. I don't know their story, but I, personally, think it's because they're too much alike."

Abel nodded. "So, other than them, everyone gets along?"

Quincy nodded with a thoughtful look on his face. "Yeah, pretty much."

The rest of the evening was consumed by eating dinner and trying to get all the boys settled in and the like. Sarah and Keturah stayed for a few more hours and then left. Abel and the boys exchanged stories and chatted until they were all exhausted from the long day and drifted off to sleep.

It felt weird to Abel to have so many people stay with him; he was so used to the solitude. The room was filled with the sounds of the soft, rhythmic breathing of the sleeping boys. And someone's snoring. Abel was pretty sure that it was Austin. He smiled to himself; it was nice to not be alone. To have friends.

CHAPTER 36

"He's waking up," someone whispered.

"He stopped thrashing," another voice noted in a hushed tone.

Abel peeled his eyes open and found himself surrounded by a semicircle of boys. He was wrapped up in his sheets and coated in sweat.

Lee, who was staring at him with wide eyes, said, "Abel, you okay?"

Abel pressed his eyes shut for a moment and tried to ignore his pounding headache.

"We were trying to wake you up," Justin explained. "You were having some sort of fit in your sleep."

Abel reopened his eyes. "I was having a nightmare."

Someone towards the back of the boys snickered. Peter glared at whoever it was and said, "Shut up," which, to Abel, seemed out of character for him.

"What was it about?" asked Quincy. "Sometimes talking makes it better."

The walls were closing in. Closer, closer, suffocating him. So tight that he couldn't move.

"Abel?" Justin said, snapping him back to reality. "Are you okay?"

A glass panel in front of him; he still couldn't move, but now he could see out. Harley stood in front of him with wide, doe-like eyes.

"He's unresponsive," Jesse said. "What do we do?"

"We can't go to get help," Austin reasoned.

"We have to do something," Matthew argued.

A person without a face approached her. "You have two choices: save the man in that room or save yourself."

"Well, what are we supposed to do?" William wondered.

"What about the HSD?" Gabriel offered.

"The what?"

"The HSD. Weren't you listening when Abel was telling his story?" Gabriel repeated.

"NO! Harley, don't do it! Save yourself!"

"Who do we send?" Garrett asked.

"Justin," Isaiah instantly replied.

"I—I—take me. Save him."

"Are you sure?" the faceless person asked.

"Where is it?" Lee examined.

"Look through his bag," Austin offered.

Abel banged against the glass, trying to get their attention. "No, Harley! No. It isn't worth it."

"I'm sure," Harley said, determination gracing her features.

Jesse grabbed Abel's backpack and dumped all of its contents onto the floor. Sifting through it all, he came across a small device. "Is this it?" he asked.

"How are we supposed to know?" Isaiah snapped.

"Not the time, guys," Quincy scolded.

Abel banged harder against the glass. Maybe he could break it. BOOM! The gunshot jolted him. He looked up just in time to see that the bullet didn't hit

Harley, but the ground at her feet. Abel was just about to sigh in relief when the floor underneath her disappeared and Harley hung comically in the air for a moment before dropping into the nothingness in slow motion.

"How does it work?" Matthew wondered, taking the small device out of Jesse's hands.

"Try pressing that button," Garrett ordered.

Abel's head pounded and his heart was racing. His breathing was labored and uneven. His eyes rolled back into his head and he began convulsing slightly.

"Guys," Austin said, pointing at Abel, "something's happening."

"Is he going into shock?" Jesse speculated.

"He did have a head and neck injury," Lee said sheepishly.

"We don't have time to get someone. Garrett, you go get Abel's mom," Justin delegated. "Peter, I need you to make sure he keeps breathing; check at least every five minutes. If he stops, alert William immediately; he knows CPR. William, stand by. Austin, check his pulse. Jesse, I want you to go into the bathroom and get a wet washcloth. Lee, grab all the blankets you can get and put them on Abel; we need to keep him warm."

"I thought you were supposed to lift the legs if they're going into shock," Isaiah said.

"Not if you suspect head, neck, or back injury," Justin denied.

The boys had already dispersed, doing what Justin had told them to. "What do I do with the washcloth?" Jesse asked.

"Put it on his forehead. Try not to move his head at all," Justin commanded as he tried to loosen the blankets that Abel had gotten tied up in during his nightmare without moving Abel. "Do we have any scissors or something in here?"

"I have my knife," Isaiah offered.

"Perfect," Justin said, accepting the sharp object and cutting off Abel's sheets. "That should help his circulation."

"I got the thicker blankets," Lee said.

"Great. Help me place them around him carefully. Do *not* move him *at all* and do *not* tuck them in *at all*," Justin commanded. "Pulse, Austin?"

"Weak and erratic," Austin reported.

"Breathing, Peter?"

"Labored but consistent."

"Where is Garrett with Sarah?" Matthew muttered.

Just as he said it, the two came running in. "Abel," Sarah cried out with tears streaming down her face.

"How's he doing?" Garrett asked.

"The same," Justin told him. "Hopefully he'll improve soon. There isn't much that I can do to be honest. Without a corticosteroid of some sort, there is absolutely nothing we can do."

"Then Abel's going to die?" Sarah asked, near hysterics.

Justin looked at the floor. "Without the corticosteroid to help reduce the swelling on the spinal cord? Yes."

"Oh my god. Abel, I'm here. Abel, sweetie, wake up, I'm here for you."

"Pulse?" Justin asked Austin again.

"Still weak and erratic. It's slightly decreased in speed."

"Breathing?"

"He's still breathing; it's less labored," Peter informed.

"Where is the nearest hospital?" Jesse asked.

"We can't take him to a hospital; they'll kill him." Isaiah scoffed. "Not to mention that we can't leave without being killed either."

"That's not what I meant, idiot," Jesse glared. "If there's a hospital nearby, we could sneak in and steal some corti–whatever–thingy—"

"Corticosteroid," Justin corrected.

"That's what I said. Anyways, we could sneak in, steal some and bring it back to Abel."

"That's not a bad plan. Sarah, where's the nearest hospital? We need to administer a corticosteroid within eight hours of the beginning of going into shock. It's been about forty minutes," Justin said.

"How do you know all this?" Sarah asked through her tears.

"Each one of us was trained to be an EMT for a certain part of the body. That way if anyone got injured while we were on a mission, we could treat him," Justin explained. "I got delegated the best one: the brain."

"Not the time for sarcasm," Garrett reminded.

"Right. Hospitals?"

"The closest one is about ten minutes from here," Sarah told the boys.

"We need a small strike team to infiltrate the hospital. The corticosteroid would be stored in the emergency department. Volunteers?"

"Well, we obviously need Abel's mom," Austin said. "And you need to stay here to monitor Abel along with William since he knows CPR. I have to stay to monitor his heartbeat and Peter needs to monitor his breathing. That leaves Garrett, Isaiah, Quincy, Lee, Matthew, Gabriel, and Jesse."

"I want no more than five people going on this mission," Justin ordered. "And we need some way to keep in touch."

"I'll go," Lee offered. "It was my fault anyways."

"And me," Garrett said. He didn't state his reasons, but it was implied that he would be the leadership on the mission.

"I'll go too," Quincy volunteered.

"That leaves Isaiah, Gabriel, Matthew, and Jesse."

"Gabe will stay with me," William said. "He's lungs. We might need him."

"I'll go," Matthew whispered.

A wave of shock rolled over everyone, but no one said anything. "Okay," Justin agreed. "That'll be five. Jesse, Isaiah, you can help me try to keep Abel warm and stable. Sarah, a way for us to stay in contact?"

"I have my HoloCom; I can hook it up to the security system that Keturah has in here."

"How would I work it?"

"It'll monitor everything you say and transmit it to me. I'll set it so that if you say my name, it'll activate."

Justin nodded. "You have a little less than seven hours. Let's get this done, people. Time is of the essence."

CHAPTER 37

Sarah led the four boys through the pitch black forest. The silence was deafening and the emotions were running high. "Just a little further," she assured the boys in a whisper.

The lights of the giant glass building penetrated the thick canopy of trees. Sarah stopped and held her arm out to stop the boys. "This is it," she whispered. "The emergency department is the building closest to where we are now. When I get inside, I'll sneak into the storage room and get masks, hats, and scrubs for you all to put on, and, if I can, a gurney. That'll give us instant access to the medicine storage. I'll meet you back here so that you can change into the clothes and then we'll infiltrate as a team. Questions?"

No one said anything. "Okay, I'll be back within forty minutes. No one move and make no noises. If someone comes this way, retreat farther into the woods."

The boys nodded and Sarah watched them for a moment as they sat down onto the ground. "If I'm not back within forty minutes...no. I'll be back within forty minutes."

Sarah glanced back once more before departing down the thick foliage towards the bright lights of the hospital. The emergency department was right in front of her. They were in the middle of rushing around to get some patient in, and through the hustle and bustle, they didn't even notice Sarah slip in.

She walked briskly down the long, white main hallway. The fumes of bleach filled her nostrils. The hallway was empty and silent; her footsteps echoed on the tiled, white floors. Where are the gurneys and operating supplies kept?

Sarah opened the door to what appeared to be a closet. Score! It was filled with all the scrubs and masks that she'd ever need. Now she only needed to find a gurney.

She'd come back for the supplies, she decided. She glanced up and down the hallway. Still abandoned. Almost no one could afford health care anymore.

Sarah took a deep breath, trying to stabilize her pounding heart. She trotted down the hallway and took a left; she was pretty sure that this led to the main entrance where the ambulances pulled up. She poked head around another corner and saw four people running with a stretcher down the hallway. She sucked in a breath and turned her head slightly so no one could see her face. As soon as the ladies with the stretcher had passed Sarah, she rushed to the main entrance and grabbed the gurney that they had abandoned. Running back up the hallway with the gurney, she got back to the supply closet and bundled the clothes up and then laid a blanket over it to make it look like a body.

Ready to make her escape back to the woods, Sarah turned and began pushing the gurney towards the back exit where she had originally come in at. She halted in her tracks when she saw Mazy, the head nurse, making her way down the hall.

"Sarah!" she greeted. "What are you doing here?"

"I, uh, volunteer here sometimes."

"What're you doing with that gurney?" Mazy asked, sounding slightly suspicious.

"I'm taking it to the morgue," Sarah lied smoothly, trying not to display the fear she felt.

"The morgue is in the opposite direction," Mazy said.

"Oh...." Sarah replied trying to think of a good lie. "Well, I just started volunteering and this is a pretty large hospital, so sometimes I get lost."

Mazy smiled understandingly. "Down that hall, take a left, then a right. You'll see two different sets of doors; go to the one on the right and then go down that hall and take another left."

"Left, right, right door, hall, left?" Sarah asked, playing along.

"Yes."

"Thank you," Sarah said, taking off in the direction. She was sure that there'd be an exit along the way.

She glanced over her shoulder frequently to make sure that no one was behind her. She took the left, the right, and then stopped at the two sets of doors. One had a sign that said "to morgue" and the other had a sign that said "exit". Sarah took the exit and found herself in an abandoned parking lot.

She hurried across it and into the forest. She tried to figure out how far away she was from the boys; Sarah figured that she was at least a hundred yards from their position. She trekked carefully through the dense tree line, trying to make it back to the boys. She heard hushed voices to her left that fell silent as they heard the crunching of the leaves.

"Sarah?" a voice asked.

"It's me," she whispered back.

Sarah made her way over to where they were sitting. "I got the stuff."

Garrett stood and grabbed a pair of scrubs from the gurney, throwing it to Matthew. "Get changed," he ordered the boys, throwing more scrubs at them.

Sarah grabbed a pair and changed too. When they had all put on their masks and little hats, Sarah asked, "Who's getting in the gurney? It can't be me."

"Who looks the least like a girl?" Lee offered.

"Lee," Matthew decided. "You're the oldest and largest."

Garrett glared at Matthew, but didn't dispute his decision. Lee climbed into the gurney and pulled the blanket up over his head. "The emergency entrance is to the right slightly. I'll do all the talking. Our story is that there was an accident and the patient has to be rushed to the operating room. No one can disturb us in the operating room. They should have a small storage room attached to the OR with things like IVs, medicine, and stuff like that. Ready?" Sarah said.

Everyone nodded. "Let's go."

Sarah led the way out of the trees with Garrett and Quincy pushing the gurney. Sarah was pulling it along at the front and Matthew was on the left side. The sliding doors of the main emergency entrance slid open, permitting them to run down a hallway with a nurse trailing them. "What's the emergency?"

"Accident. We need to operate immediately," Sarah told the nurse.

"OR 5 is prepped for operation," the nurse informed.

"Thank you. That'll be all," Sarah dismissed.

The nurse stopped running alongside the gurney and allowed Sarah to lead, turning left. "There's a map ahead," Sarah muttered.

They halted at said map and Sarah inspected it. "OR 5 is this way," she determined, pointing down the hall that they had turned into.

They rushed down the hallway a little farther and Sarah steered them: left, left, right. "Third door on the left," she told the boys.

They turned into it and locked the door. Lee immediately hopped off the gurney. "Open all the closets. It has to be here somewhere," Garrett instructed.

The boys began scouring every inch of the room. "I found an IV," Lee announced.

"Does it have saline bags with it?" Sarah questioned.

"Yeah."

"Put it by the gurney," Sarah told Lee as she searched through a storage closet.

"I found where they keep the medicine!" Matthew cheered. "One problem though: they're labeled by their brand names, not corticosteroid."

"Contact Justin," Garrett ordered.

Sarah pulled out her HoloCom and turned it on. "Justin, this is Sarah. We're in the hospital, but we need the exact drug name."

There was a bunch of shouting in the background and Justin shouted, "Look for dexamethasone, glucocorticoid, or prednisolone. Those are all anti-inflammatories in the corticosteroid family."

There were more ruckuses in the background and Justin said, "Abel's having severe bradycardia; we have less time than we thought. Maybe five hours. Tops. We need you to also get...Will, what drug do we need?"

"Atropine, epinephrine, or dopamine," William supplemented.

"Matthew?" Sarah prompted.

"I see dexamethasone and prednisolone and glucocorticoid, so I'm grabbing all of those; still looking for the atropine, epinephrine, and dopamine."

Garrett shoved him to the side slightly. "Let me see."

"You looking won't make a difference," Matthew snapped.

"Boys!" Justin scolded through the HoloCom.

"I found it!" Quincy exclaimed from across the room.

"Do we need anything else?" Sarah asked Justin.

"If there's any way that you can snag a heart monitor and a...what did you need, Gabriel?"

"An oxygen mask...."

"There might be some in here; we could hook it up to Lee to make it look more realistic when we sneak back out," Quincy said.

"Okay, gotta go," Justin said. There was a click and the noise died.

"I found the oxygen and heart monitor," Lee announced. "Let's bounce."

Sarah ushered Lee onto the bed and strapped the oxygen mask to his face, attached the heart monitor to him and handed him the IV tube. "I'm not going to turn any of it on, but I need you to hold it."

Sarah pulled the blanket over his head again and they hurried out of the operating room. They hadn't expected for anyone to be waiting outside the door, let alone twenty hospital staff.

CHAPTER 38

As soon as Sarah had left, the complications began. "His pulse is dropping!" Austin screamed.

"Move," Will ordered, pushing past Austin and feeling Abel's pulse. "It's well below sixty!"

He began pumping his hands on Abel's chest, trying to keep his heart beating at around sixty. "How's his breathing?" William asked.

"Still pretty good," Peter reported.

"Gabe," William said, "check just to make sure he's getting enough oxygen. His nails are turning slightly blue."

Gabriel sat next to Peter and began examining Abel's nails, pressing his ear to Abel's lungs, and laying his cheek next to Abel's nose.

"His breathing could be better," Gabriel admitted, "but for now it's fine."

"He's losing heat," Jesse reported to Justin.

"Shit," Justin swore under his breath. "We need to keep him warm."

"What should we do?" Jesse wondered.

"Let me think," Justin said, pacing back and forth slightly. "We've insulated him the best we can with the thick blankets; that should help keep his body temperature up, but it's still dropping. What to do...? That's it!"

"What?" asked Jesse.

"You and Isaiah take a side and lay next to him. Hopefully he'll absorb some of your body heat."

They looked like they wanted to argue, but after one glance to Abel's lifeless-looking body, they climbed in on either side of the bed.

William stopped pumping and grabbed Abel's wrist, checking his pulse again. "He's stabilized slightly."

"Breathing?" Justin asked.

"He's still good," Gabriel said.

Without warning, William began pumping again. "Call Sarah," William ordered. "Tell her that we need—"

Before he could finish, Sarah's voice filled the room. "Justin, this is Sarah. We're in the hospital, but we need the exact drug name."

William was telling Gabe something, causing him to dart around the room in search of something and Jesse was talking to Austin. "Look for dexamethasone, glucocorticoid, or prednisolone. Those are all anti-inflammatories in the corticosteroid family."

"Tell her about the bradycardia," William ordered.

"Abel's having severe bradycardia; we have less time than we thought. Maybe five hours. Tops. We need you to also get...Will, what drug do we need?"

"Atropine, epinephrine, or dopamine," William said while still pumping away.

"Matthew," Sarah said on the other end of the line.

"I see dexamethasone and prednisolone and glucocorticoid, so I'm grabbing all of those; still looking for the atropine, epinephrine, and dopamine."

"Let me see," Garrett demanded

"You looking won't make a difference," Matthew snapped.

"Boys!" Justin scolded

"I found it!" Quincy shouted.

"Do we need anything else?" Sarah asked Justin.

"If there's any way that you can snag a heart monitor and a...what did you need, Gabriel?"

"An oxygen mask...." Gabriel said as he lowered his head to Abel's nose again.

"There might be some in here; we could hook it up to Lee to make it look more realistic when we sneak back out," Quincy said.

"Okay, gotta go," Justin said as he noticed William gesturing for him to come over.

"How's his temperature?" Justin asked Jesse and Isaiah.

"Better, I think," Isaiah and Jesse said at the same time. They both glared at each other.

"How long do you think we have?" Justin asked Will.

"No more than four hours now. His heart rate won't stay level. It'll drop dramatically and then pick back up. That isn't good for his body."

"What about you, Gabe?"

"He might have five hours until the lack of oxygen gets to him. His breathing isn't too bad right now, but...."

Justin nodded and prayed that Sarah and the boys would be back soon. They didn't have any time to waste.

CHAPTER 39

Stay calm, Sarah told herself. "Can we help you?" asked Sarah in her most even tone.

"We'd like to see the patient," Mazy said.

"That isn't a good idea right not. She shouldn't be exposed due to her lack of body heat."

Mazy pressed her lips together. "You look familiar."

"I get that a lot," Sarah falsely admitted, trying to disguise her voice slightly.

Mazy gave a skeptical look, but moved to let them pass. It took every effort for Sarah not to let out a sigh of relief. They began to walk down the hallway and the staff began dispersing.

"Wait!" Mazy called out to Sarah.

"Keep going," she told the boys. "I'll meet back up with you later."

The boys gave her a look, but kept moving. Sarah turned to face Mazy. "Yes?"

"Sarah? Is that you?"

Sarah momentarily closed her eyes; she had to buy the boys some time to get out of the hospital. "Yes."

"What were you doing in the OR? Volunteers are never supposed to enter an operating room."

"I, uh, was, um...." Sarah was all out of lies.

"Were you sneaking around and stealing drugs?" Mazy exclaimed.

Sarah had no response, so Mazy took her silence as an affirmative. "I'm going to have to detain you," Mazy said.

Sarah sighed. At least the boys were well on their way. "Okay," Sarah acquiesced.

Sarah must've been mistaken, but she thought she saw...she thought she saw Mazy wink.

Mazy took Sarah's wrists and twisted her arms behind her back. "The guard changes in thirty minutes, but don't get any ideas."

Was Mazy trying to help her? "Mazy?" Sarah whispered.

"See you Monday," Mazy said into Sarah's ear. Monday? As in at the meeting?

Sarah grinned and Mazy practically yelled. "Let's go. We can't have criminals running amuck."

Mazy began transporting Sarah to the detainment room. As they approached the room, Mazy opened the door and pushed Sarah in, saying to the guard, "Caught this one stealing drugs."

"Put her over there," the guard grunted, pointing to corner of the room.

Mazy shoved Sarah into the corner and gave her one last wink. "Thanks, Gertrude," Mazy said before exiting.

Sarah stood in wait for thirty minutes when the guards changed. The lady, Gertrude, gave Sarah one final glare and then left, the door slowly shutting behind her. Sarah rushed over and grabbed the door just before it shut all the way and quietly snuck down the hallway to her right, breaking into a run when she was sure that Gertrude wouldn't be able to hear her.

When she got back to the woods, Sarah could hear loud arguing.

"I'm saying this for the last time. We. Should. Go. Back," Matthew shouted.

"And get ourselves killed not to mention Abel? I told you, Mattie, no. We have to get back to HQ," Garrett argued.

"What about Sarah? What do you think they'll do to her?"

"Mattie, I—"

"How about a compromise?" Quincy offered. "Half goes back and the other half takes the supplies to Justin."

"Or how about we all go back to HQ?" Sarah interjected.

All four boys jumped and turned to face Sarah. "What—how—?" Matthew gaped.

"Let's go," Sarah urged.

CHAPTER 40

Justin was just about to contact Sarah again when all five people burst through the door, pushing a gurney, with an IV, heart monitor, and oxygen machine. He sprang into action. William had been helping Abel's heart for the last thirty minutes and had to occasionally, on Gabriel's orders, give a few puffs of oxygen. Jesse and Isaiah had enlisted the help of Austin and Peter to keep Abel warm.

If the five noticed anything odd about the four people squeezed into bed with Abel, they didn't comment.

Justin ordered Gabriel to hook up the IV as he put the heart monitor onto him turned it on; the beeping noise emitted was slow and almost painful to hear. Beep...... beep...... beep.......

After inserting the IV into Abel's vein, Gabriel hooked up the oxygen mask, strapping it on Abel. Just by doing that the beeps increased slightly. Beep..... beep..... beep......

Justin hurried to the gurney and took the vials of medicine, grabbing the dexamethasone. He attached it to the IV and it began dripping along with the saline fluid.

"How many bags of saline did you grab?" Justin asked.

"Enough for a month," Sarah reported, going to her son's side.

Justin nodded and watched as the vial drained. As soon as it was empty he had Gabriel hand him one of the drugs for Abel's heart, the dopamine. Justin attached that one to Abel's IV and let it slowly drip into his veins.

Beep.... beep.... beep....

"We should have one person keep watch at all times," Justin announced. "Everyone else needs to get some sleep; I'll take first watch."

Justin was scared by how close it had been. He didn't want to tell Sarah, but it had been touch and go for the last forty minutes. Any longer and Abel probably wouldn't have made it. Justin was impressed that he had survived that long; Abel certainly was a fighter.

Everyone else had dispersed and fallen asleep (Justin was pretty sure that Peter, Austin, Jesse, and Isaiah were all asleep next to Abel). Justin sat in the chair next to Abel and placed his head in his hands. The stress and pressure that had rested on him for the past three hours made its way to the surface and Justin sat there, letting a few tears drip down his cheeks. Beep... beep... beep....

Justin couldn't help the grin that spread across his face. He looked at the heart monitor: sixty beats a minute.

CHAPTER 41

Abel peeled his eyes open and immediately the headache hit. Not only the headache, but the dizziness. He shut his eyes again and took a deep breath. Someone stirred next to him and Abel reopened his eyes to see Justin leaning over on a chair with his elbows resting on his knees.

"He's awake! He's awake! Sarah! Jesse, Matthew! Someone! Oh my god, you're awake."

"Not so loud," Abel croaked.

"Abel's awake?" Austin exclaimed upon entering the bedroom. "Thank everything that is good in the universe! Abel!"

"Not so loud," Abel repeated.

"I'll go get Sarah and the guys!" Austin cheered in a hushed tone.

"You guys act like I was dying," Abel muttered.

Justin gave him a solemn, severe look. Before Abel could respond, the boys and Sarah came rushing in. "Abel! Are you okay? How do you feel?"

"I'm fine mom. It was only a nightmare."

Sarah gave him an odd look and glanced at Justin. "He doesn't remember anything."

"Remember what?" Abel asked.

"There isn't much to remember; he passed out before anything happened," Jesse reminded.

"Remember what?" Abel repeated, trying to curb the headache and nausea.

"You've been out for over a week," Justin told him. "You *did* almost die. You went into neurogenic shock from the blow to the head and neck that you took the day we got here."

Abel frowned. "I what?"

"Went into neurogenic shock. Medical terms, blah, blah, blah, the point is your heart almost stopped beating and you almost stopped breathing and you've been in a coma for the past week," Justin informed.

"God, my head hurts," Abel murmured.

"Do we have any pain meds?" Justin asked Sarah.

Matthew shuffled through the vials that they had grabbed from the hospital. "I accidentally grabbed some hydrocodone when I was looking for the corticosteroids."

"Vicodin?" Justin analyzed. "That'll work. This is going to make you sleepy, Abel."

Needless to say the two weeks of recovery sucked. For the first half, Abel's head was pounding and he wasn't allowed to get out of bed and for the second half, Justin allowed him to take short walks to the bathroom and back, but not unassisted. Abel was closely monitored at all times and only when Justin was sure that Abel had fully recovered, were the heart monitor and IV removed.

When Abel was finally on his feet again, he felt like everyone was being super careful around him. Like he was made of glass, about to break at any moment. He also felt like he had missed a lot of key bonding and such. He felt like an outsider around the guys even though they strived to make him feel included. Even Garret and Matthew were getting along better.

Just before the meeting on Monday, Abel approached Keturah. "I think we should free the people that were imprisoned for fighting for male rights."

"That was actually the topic we were going over this week. Justin suggested it," she told him.

"Oh."

Abel tried not to feel angry or jealous. He was being petty. All that mattered was the people needed to be freed.

But he couldn't help but feel replaced.

Abel shook his head. The anger welled up in his chest and he wanted to kick something. Jealousy coursed through his veins.

"That's...good."

"Are you feeling okay, Abel?" Keturah asked.

"I'm feeling...fine."

He was feeling anything but fine, but he didn't want anyone to think he was being trivial.

Keturah gave him an unsure smile and asked him to take a seat. She opened the meeting with the usual statements and then asked Justin to stand.

"We are going to free all those who were thrown in jail fighting for what they believe in. The government has a special jail just for them; sometimes we had to guard it. We know all the weaknesses and where everyone is kept. Tomorrow is normally visiting day for family members. It's when the security is at its lowest. Visiting hours are between seven and two. Just after two, the guards escort the prisoners back to their cells. That's when we strike."

He even sounded like a better leader than Abel. He didn't say "um" once and he was so sure of himself. Abel hated himself for thinking these things. He was being stupid.

The audience cheered loudly and Justin sat back down with a charming smile gracing his face. Peter slid into the chair next to Abel. "Hey," he whispered.

Abel nodded in response.

"Are you okay? You've been acting weird since you woke up."

Even Peter had changed so much in three weeks. He was so much less timid these days.

"I'm fine."

Peter gave Abel a look. "Come on. You can tell me; I won't tell anyone."

Abel studied Peter for a moment before saying. "Three weeks and I'm replaced."

"What?"

"Three weeks and I'm replaced. Was I ever even needed?"

"Abel, do you understand how much Justin looks up to you?" Peter looked at his lap with a blush forming on his cheeks. "How much I look up to you?"

Abel stayed silent. "Justin's always talking about how amazing you are, surviving three hours with under sixty beats a minute.... He's always been in a position of leadership; you got thrown into it a few months ago and you've succeeded with flying colors. Abel, you've done in a few months, more than what some people do in their entire lives. We admire you endlessly and one of the reasons that a lot of us are so standoffish towards you is because we are embarrassed that we admire you so much. Justin is trying to impress *you*."

Abel met Peter's eyes. Finally a grin made its way to Abel's face. "Thank you, Peter. I was being stupid."

"No," Peter corrected, "you were being human."

Abel smiled at Peter and shoved his shoulder. Peter grinned back with a small blush blooming across his neck.

CHAPTER 42

Justin approached Abel the next day just before the incursion. "I want you to lead the attack," he said, not meeting Abel's eyes.

Abel grinned at him. "Why don't you do it, Justin? You are the one who put all the work into it."

Justin blanched and jerked his eyes up to meet Abel's. "I couldn't. You—I—uh..."

Abel grinned. "You put all the work into it while in the middle of saving my life. You deserve this."

Justin's blanch quickly turned to a blush. He didn't say anything, but stared at Abel with admiration evident in his eyes.

"Come on," Abel prompted. "We have an hour and a half; you should probably give your inspirational speech."

Justin opened and closed his mouth like a goldfish and Abel laughed, turning and walking to the meeting room with Justin trailing behind him.

When they got there, Justin had managed to compose himself. He stood in front of the volunteers for the strike, including Sarah, Keturah, all of the men, and a few others from the meetings. "Today is the first step of many, the first battle to be won; freeing all those before us who have been prosecuted for standing up for what they believed in. Today we make a stand when all others have taken a seat. Failure is not an option nor is it a possibility. We will win!"

Cheers went up around Abel, and Abel sent Justin a reassuring grin.

Justin smiled confidently and led everyone into the forest. "The prison isn't far from here. Funnily enough, they hid it in the woods too."

Justin walked in silence for a few more minutes and then stopped abruptly. "It's just ahead."

Abel could barely make out a barbed wire fence rising above the canopy.

"If we go around back, we can sneak in the back entrance and hide. There are sixty cells. After they bring the prisoners back in, Maria is going to hack into the security system," he said, motioning to a lady that was standing close by.

Abel instantly thought of Harley and how good she would've been at hacking the system.

"After Maria hacks the security, everyone takes four cells and escorts the people safely into the woods and back to HQ. Let's go."

Justin led the way around the prison to the back of the building. "We're going to have to go over the wall. During visiting hours, they have the wall's security turned off so we have to be fast."

Abel volunteered to go first, finding a foothold in the giant wall. He pulled himself up and felt his arms burning already. Finding another foothold as quickly as possible, he propelled himself up a little higher. His arms shook as he tried to find a higher spot to put his hands. There was a small ledge-like thing where only Abel's fingertips fit, but it was all he had. He grabbed it and tried to pull himself up, putting his feet where his hands had previously been. He felt his fingers slipping and panicked, looking for a different place to put his hands. He was pretty close to the top. Abel stretched and tried to reach the top of the wall; he'd have to jump to reach it, but there was nothing else to grab onto. Abel took a deep breath and pushed off the wall, grasping at the very top.

He heard everyone gasp from below; he tried to tune them out as his legs dangled freely beneath him. He'd have to pull himself all the way up. Abel's arms were already sore and burning and they trembled as they struggled to hold his entire body weight. He bent his legs as he strained to pull his chin over the edge of the wall. Abel somehow (perhaps the imminent thought of falling to his death) managed to get his forearms over the top and get more leverage to hoist himself up. After what seemed like a lifetime, Abel lifted his leg up to the ledge on the wall and stood.

He laid his jacket over the barbed wire, swung a leg over and then the other. He dropped to his knees and lowered himself into a dangling position once more after checking to make sure that no one was coming. Abel struggled to find a foothold, kicking against the wall until finally he got traction. He slowly lowered himself switching from foothold to foothold and handhold to hand hold until he was only about seven feet off the ground. Then he just jumped and surprisingly landed on his feet.

Abel glanced around to make sure no one was coming and then gave Justin the signal to send someone else over, whistling loudly. The signal that someone was coming was kicking the wall.

Abel waited a few minutes before seeing Jesse's head pop over the wall. He carefully began lowering himself over the wall. He was about three feet down from the top when his grip slipped and his mouth formed a small 'o' as he plummeted towards the ground.

Abel's eyes widened. He couldn't just let Jesse fall. He rushed forward and held out his arms to catch him. Surprisingly enough, Jesse landed in Abel's arms, but his weight plus his momentum sent both boys toppling to the ground. "You okay?" Abel asked.

Jesse closed his eyes, let out a shaky breath, and nodded.

Abel whistled again and over came Gabriel. And then Peter, and Isaiah, Quincy, William, Matthew, Austin, Garrett, then Lee. Next was Abel's mom, who he helped down, Keturah, he also helped her, Mazy, some other woman, a girl he was pretty sure was named Nicole, and the hacker, Maria. He helped all the ladies. Lastly, Justin climbed over the wall, lowering himself down smoothly and glancing around the area.

"The back entrance is over here. What's the time?"

Sarah glanced at her watch. "Two till."

"Okay, when I say go, we're all going to cross the courtyard and open the back door. The security system that's wired to the entrances and exits of the building are also turned off during visiting hours. We have to time this precisely. Time?"

"Still two till. Wait, one till."

"Go!" Justin urged.

They all crossed the courtyard and Justin cracked open the door just enough so that you wouldn't notice from the inside.

He put a finger to his lips, indicating to be silent. Abel thought about the poor security of the prison; it had been so easy to get in. But he guessed that it wouldn't be easy if you didn't have inside information like they did. They could hear the guards putting the prisoners back in their containment units and slowly the noise died away.

"I'll go first," Justin whispered.

He slunk into the jail and after a few moments poked his head out. "Come on in, guys."

Everyone followed him in and Abel took the time to look around a little. It was all white with bright lights and the cells that Abel could see only had one person apiece and had what looked like glass separating the prisoners from the hallway.

"The control panel is over here," Justin whispered to Sarah. She nodded and silently walked over to where Justin was and began working on the security.

The people that were nearest to Abel were all standing at the glass, watching the group suspiciously. Some were young and some were old, but they all looked like they wanted out. The closest lady to Abel looked about his mother's age. Bruises lined her face, neck, and arms, and there was a nasty gash that ran from her lip to her forehead. Long, ratty blonde hair circled her shoulders and blue eyes pierced his own. He looked at the embroidered name on her jumpsuit: Haim.

Abel's heart sped up slightly and he met her eyes again, trying to convey some unspoken message. Her eyes were wide and confused and even a little wild, but she looked so innocent. It hurt Abel's heart.

The glass panels lifted up and retracted into the ceiling in one swift swoosh. "I want four of you to go with each person quietly and calmly," Justin whispered. "We're here to help you and will explain everything later."

All the women nodded. Abel grabbed Harley's mom's arm and steered her with him, taking three other women. "This way," Abel whispered.

He led them out the back exit and motioned to the wall. "We're going to have to climb up. I'll help you."

The women's faces were stony with determination. None of them looked deterred. Abel lifted the first lady up as high as he could and let her use his hands as footholds for as long as he could. After she disappeared over the other side, Abel did the same with the next and the next until he got to Mrs. Haim who had positioned herself in the back on purpose, letting the other women escape first. Abel stared into her eyes for a few seconds; she looked just like Harley. "I'm Abel," he whispered into her ear as he lifted her up. "I'm in love with your daughter."

She didn't react that Abel could see; she just seemed determined to top the wall. After she disappeared over the other side, Abel began climbing over. He dropped down next to Mrs. Haim and was immediately wrapped in a hug. "When do I get to see her? When do I get to see Harley?"

Abel squirmed uncomfortably, not knowing what to say. Instead he just shook his head and said, "I'll explain later."

Mrs. Haim smiled at him and nodded.

Abel couldn't help but smile back at her. She was very amiable. She was so much like Harley. More people began to hop over the wall and Abel quickly went to help them, momentarily distracted from Harley's mom. Justin was the last one over again. He motioned for them to retreat into the woods and once they were a safe distance away said, "When we get back to HQ, I'll explain everything. I'm sure you're all confused. I know I was."

They marched in silence for the rest of the way back to the meeting room which gave Abel plenty of time to think. The problem was that there was nothing to think about. It felt like all Abel had done lately was think and now he let his mind wander. He managed to stay with the group as they wandered through the woods, back to the underground hideout. When everyone had settled into a chair in the circular room, Justin took the front of the room and gestured for Abel to join him.

"So I know you guys are probably confused; I think Abel should explain."

Abel blinked and then started telling the story that he had come so accustomed to telling. Towards the end, Justin and/or Keturah interjected occasionally, but mostly they let Abel explain. After he had wrapped up, Keturah took a step forward.

"So obviously there isn't room for everyone here. Half of you will be coming with me to Bunker B and the other half will go with Sarah to Bunker C."

"You have more bunkers?" Abel asked.

Keturah smirked at him. "Well, you didn't think I'd put all my eggs in one basket, did you?"

Abel tilted his head. He wasn't quite sure what that meant, but he assumed that she was just saying yes in an odd way. Keturah counted the people off, half going with Abel's mom and the other half going with Keturah. The other ladies who had assisted in the jailbreak didn't go back to the bunker with Abel, the boys, Keturah, Sarah, and the jailbirds, opting to go back to work instead as to raise less suspicion.

When all the ladies were about to leave, Abel pulled aside Mrs. Haim. "Harley died saving my life," Abel admitted, deciding not to beat around the bush.

Mrs. Haim pressed her eyes closed and when she reopened them there was actually a little twinkle in them. "Saving you, eh? I always knew Harley was a hero, but I didn't foresee that. Then again, she was always very selfless and very stubborn."

Abel didn't really know what to say, but Mrs. Haim went on talking, "Thank you."

She didn't specify what she was thanking him for, but turned and left with the rest of the women.

That meant it was just Abel and the guys.

"So what do you guys want to do tonight?" Austin asked.

"Relax for once," Jesse scoffed.

Abel grinned. "Anyone know how to play poker?"

They all gave him blank looks and he grinned wider. Motioning for them to follow, he walked back to the bedroom and pulled out the deck of cards that his mother had given him during his recovery. He shuffled, dealt five cards to everyone, and began explaining the rules.

A few rounds later they decided they were okay enough to try doing it with bets; stupid things like whoever lost had to put a pair of the winner's underwear on their head and so on and so forth. Abel won most of the rounds, but it was fun nonetheless. Isaiah grumbled through most of it, but Abel could tell that he was enjoying himself too. Lee ended up losing most of the games because he was way too ambitious for his own good.

When everyone finally got tired of poker, Abel moved on to teach them more card games like Bullshit, Old Maid, Go Fish (Harley's favorite), Blackjack, Gin Rummy, and Crazy Eights. Abel normally won these, too, but he discovered that Gabriel was actually pretty good at picking up all the rules and, given a few more rounds, would probably be beating Abel. Abel was never very good at card games anyway.

They were playing one last round of Go Fish when the alarms began blaring (Keturah had increased security after the boys had managed to infiltrate the facility so easily). Justin swore under his breath and the boys abandoned their cards to go see what was going on. Abel took the front and cautiously inspected the living room, bathroom, and finally the meeting room.

"What was that?" Jesse whispered.

"What?" Austin asked bewilderedly.

"That noise...."

"I didn't hear anything."

"Me either."

"Shush...." Abel scolded before an argument broke out among the boys, a commonplace.

Abel strained his ears to listen to whatever Jesse had heard. Silence stretched out across the entire room, but then.... Footsteps coming down the stairs. Keturah had the security system set to recognize everyone in the rebellion. Abel turned to Justin and whispered, "Take the boys and hide in the bathroom. Lock the doors and each of you go into a stall, locking that door too. Don't come out until I get you."

"No way!" Austin objected. "We aren't leaving you."

Abel gave him a hard look and Jesse crossed his arms. "For once, the buffoon is right. We aren't leaving you."

"We don't have time to argue about this," Abel growled. "Do as I say."

The boys glanced at each other with wary eyes. They had never heard Abel speak so adamantly. "If you die, I'm going to kill you," Justin said finally, shaking his head. "Come on guys."

They all hesitantly made their way back into the bathroom, leaving Abel alone in the meeting hall. The footsteps echoed louder against the walls, beating in time with Abel's pounding heart. Ba-bum, ba-bum, ba-bum, ba-bum, ba-bum....

Abel braced himself as the door began to creak open. Before Abel knew what had hit him, he was on the floor with his head pounding. A face hovered over his and a scratchy voice said, "This is why you don't send men to do a woman's job."

Abel felt his hands and legs being bound with some sort of metallic substance, but he couldn't move; his legs felt jelly and his arms were numb. He let out a low groan which he also found barely possible.

"Ah, yes. The effects of the paralysis serum. It's only temporary," the lady assured. "Get him."

Abel felt a person on either side of him, hoisting him up and dragging him by his arms up the stairs and through the woods. He thought that maybe with the paralysis serum he wouldn't be able to feel pain, but he was mistaken. Each stair hit him in the stomach and the forest floor was littered with sticks and pinecones and rocks. His eyes began to droop; the effort of keeping them open was unbelievable. It felt like Abel was running a marathon. Finally, he gave into the serum and let his eyes slip shut.

CHAPTER 43

Justin ended up falling asleep waiting for Abel. He didn't think that it'd be possible to fall asleep in the stressful situation, but sometime around one he couldn't hold his eyes open anymore. He awoke to the sound of Sarah calling them for breakfast.

"Boys? Where are you? Breakfast!"

Justin groggily peeled his eyes open and immediately his heart picked up. Abel had never come and gotten them. Calm down, he thought, maybe he just forgot. But Justin knew somewhere deep inside his mind that it wasn't true. Abel wouldn't just forget to come and get them out of the bathroom.

Justin quickly opened the stall he had chosen and found all the others standing in the open area, rubbing their eyes and scratching their heads. When they met Justin's wild eyes, they snapped to attention.

"Abel," Peter breathed.

Justin hurried into the bedroom, praying that he'd be in his bed. Nothing. He hurried out to meet the boys in the circular room where Sarah was standing with a grin on her face. He wasn't here. Sarah was obviously befuddled by the boys' solemn expressions.

"Where's Abel? Is he still sleeping? He's going to miss breakfast."

Justin stayed silent and walked over to the table that sat in the middle of the room. On the table was a lone piece of paper that Justin knew hadn't been there the night before.

We've taken him. If you want him, you'll have to come and get him. You have two weeks until he's gone forever. Choose wisely, Keturah.

Chancellor Mia

Justin's eyes widened. Gone forever?

"What's wrong?" Sarah asked. "Why do you all look so depressed?"

Justin sighed. "You need to go get Keturah."

"What? Why?"

"Just do it. I'll explain everything when she gets here. I don't want to have to say this twice," Justin said.

He rubbed his forehead and Sarah nodded. "I'll be right back," she told them. "Here's your breakfast."

No one was hungry, but they all nodded and attempted a smile which probably looked a lot more like a grimace. Once Sarah was gone, Peter walked over and took the note from Justin. "What does it say?" he asked. Justin flinched and let Peter read it for himself.

" 'We've taken him. If you want him, you'll have to come and get him. You have two weeks until he's gone forever. Choose, wisely, Keturah. Chancellor Mia.'" Peter read aloud. "Gone forever?"

"Gone forever," Austin echoed.

"We have to save him!" Matthew exclaimed.

"Are you stupid?" Garrett asked, shoving Matthew slightly. "It's obviously a trap."

"Who cares?" Jesse cried. "We can't just let Abel die!"

"Be logical," Isaiah scoffed.

Jesse glared at Isaiah. "Shut up. So you're saying that to save your own skin you'd let Abel die?"

"Not just my own; yours too. And everyone else involved with this."

"Guys," Quincy scolded. "Not the time. Why can't you just get along for five seconds?"

"Stay out of this, Quincy," Isaiah barked, shoving Quincy.

"Hey!" William objected. "Leave him alone. He was just trying to be logical and helpful while all of you are losing your heads."

"No one asked you, William!" Isaiah shouted.

"*HEY*!" Justin bellowed at the top of his lungs.

All the boys stopped bickering, faced Justin, and shrunk back a little like a scolded puppy when they saw the look on Justin's face.

"This is not the time to be arguing over stupid things! We—I—have more important things to worry about than whether you guys are going to kill each other! Who cares?! Shape up or get out because I am tired of the constant bickering and fighting between you guys! We are a team and we are adults! Start acting like it!"

The boys who had been fighting stared at the floor and blushed. Isaiah bit his lip and offered his hand to Quincy who was still on the floor. Quincy took his hand and allowed Isaiah to pull him up.

"Now I want you all to apologize to each other," Justin patronized.

"What are we? Five?" Isaiah grumbled, glaring at the floor.

"Well, you sure are acting like it!" Justin scolded.

"Isaiah, I'm sorry for arguing with you," Jesse said reluctantly.

"I'm sorry for jumping in the middle," Quincy conceded with a shrug. He knew that he hadn't really done anything wrong and so did Justin, but Justin was glad that Quincy could be an adult about it.

"I'm sorry, too," William said, mimicking his brother's shrug.

"I'm sorry for jumping down your throats and for pushing you," Isaiah grumbled, still glaring at the floor.

Justin nodded approvingly and then gave Garrett a sharp look. Garrett's eyes widened and he glared at Justin. "You can't be serious."

Justin's face remained stony and Garrett sighed. "I'm sorry for calling you stupid and shoving you, Mattie," Garrett mumbled.

Matthew was about to fuss about Garrett calling him Mattie, but he caught Justin's warning look and pressed his lips together instead, clenching his jaw slightly.

Justin gave a pleased smirk and turned around to see Sarah and Keturah walking swiftly into the room. Keturah gave Justin an expectant look and he sighed, eyeing Sarah.

"You might want to sit down," he warned.

Sarah took a seat and looked like she wanted to ask questions, but she kept her mouth shut.

Justin began explaining, starting with the alarm going off, the footsteps, being told to go hide, reluctantly leaving Abel to take care of things, and ending with accidentally falling asleep, waking up, and finding the note. Keturah took the note and read over it carefully. Sarah was crying with her fist in her mouth to stifle the loud sobs.

"We should've stayed with him," Justin murmured.

Keturah shook her head. "And get yourselves captured too? Abel was very brave to sacrifice himself for you; you should be grateful."

"So when do we go to rescue him?" asked Jesse.

"We don't," Keturah stated simply.

There was an outburst of disagreements and objections, but Keturah held up her hand for silence. "It's exactly what Mia wants and exactly what she expects. It would be fifty for the price of one. They're going to torture him to try to get information and then they're going to kill him. It's as simple as that."

"But—"

"No buts," Keturah scolded with a scowl. "You think I like this? You think that I want to make this decision? I don't, but leaders have to make tough choices and they have to be for the greater good."

Justin looked over at Sarah to see how she was taking the news that they weren't going to rescue Abel. Surprisingly she had stopped crying and had a determined look set on her face. Not once did she object to Keturah's decision nor did she argue. She just sat silently. Staring off into space.

CHAPTER 44

Abel couldn't tell the difference between opening and closing his eyes; that's how dark it was. All of his belongings had been taken and his clothes had been replaced with plain, white cotton. He didn't know how long he had been sitting in the black room, but it was long enough that his stomach was rumbling and he had slept at least twice of his own free will.

His lethargy from the serum had worn off and now he was completely aware. There were only a few things Abel knew about where he was: it was silent. Always. It was small. If Abel stuck his arm out in front of himself, it would hit the other wall, if he stood his head would touch the top, and if he stretched both arms out to his sides, they would hit either wall to his left and right. It was cold. Abel was constantly shivering in the thin cotton garments that had replaced his warm jeans and thick jacket. Had there actually been any light, he would be able to see his own breath.

Abel was starving; he figured that it had been at least two days. Maybe more. He had taken to counting the seconds, the minutes, the hours. There was nothing else to occupy his mind from the ever looming imminence of death. He accepted that he was going to die. What else would whoever kidnapped him (Abel was pretty sure that it was the government) want?

At least he'd get to see Harley soon. Besides, he wasn't the only male anymore; Justin would do just fine leading the rebellion at Keturah's side. Maybe it was better this way.

He felt nasty from the times he had to go to the bathroom and couldn't hold it any longer. He had tried to contain it as much as possible by taking off his shirt and trying to absorb some of the mess and only using the back corner. The stench was unbearable though, and of course, his shirt could only absorb so much. A rash spread across his skin from being subjected to his waste and not being rinsed off.

Abel realized something was different almost immediately. He could almost feel some sort of presence. And there was some noise that Abel couldn't place too. And then it started.

His ears filled with horrible noises, screams, and crying. Images formed themselves in his brain, the worst images that his brain could conjure up. He couldn't even describe the fear and pain that filled him. He slapped his hands over his ears, but the noise didn't stop. He squeezed his eyes shut, but the images didn't leave. His head pounded and his adrenaline raced. His breathing was heavy and ragged and he was sure that he'd hyperventilate. He couldn't think, he couldn't move. Tears trickled down his cheeks and a loud scream escaped his lips. He rocked back and forth trying to steady himself.

And then as quickly as it came, it stopped. Abel curled up and cried, feeling like a child. Imprints of the images floated around in his mind and echoes of the noises bounced around his ears. When the tears finally stopped flowing, the noises and images started up again, throwing Abel into another bout of sobs, shaking, and curling up into a fetal position, hoping for it to end.

Wishing to be dead.

CHAPTER 45

Over the next few days, Abel was subjected to this on and off torture. He grew a sort of tolerance to it until he was subjected to it all day long with no breaks. Four days of continuous torment until something different happened. Light filled up Abel's tiny room, blinding him and the cold switched to hot, burning Abel's frigid skin. Abel closed his eyes and dots danced behind his lids. The sudden warm shocked his body and he began shaking instead of shivering.

And then the noises and images began again.

Abel was almost bored with them. Sure they still bothered him, but not to the extent they used to. Now he just wanted it to be over.

Whoever was controlling whatever was going on seemed to realize this because the images and noises stopped and a door that Abel didn't even know existed opened next to him. Someone grabbed his arm roughly and pulled him out of the tiny room, restraining him the instant that he was all the way out.

Abel's arms and legs were sore from being cramped into the small space and he had absolutely no energy from the lack of food. He closed his eyes as he was drug down some hallway and into a different room where he was tied to a chair.

A few minutes later a woman accompanied by six guards walked in. "Give him some water," the woman said.

One of the guards held a glass of water to his lips, purposely spilling some on his lap. As much as Abel wanted to gulp the whole thing down, he slowly sipped it as to not throw up and to conserve it seeing as he didn't know when his next chance to have water would be. It burned down his throat, but he felt like he could actually talk now. The woman in front of him also took a seat across the table that was in between them. She folded her hands in front of her and cleared her throat.

"So how was the fear chamber?"

Abel stayed silent and glared at the woman. She laughed lightly. "You don't have to answer me. We could always just throw you back in there until you die of dehydration."

Abel didn't have the energy to fight against his ties, but managed to croak, "You won't. You need me for information."

The lady gave Abel an appraising look and smiled, but it had no warmth. "You're smart. But we can put you back in the chamber until you're willing to cooperate."

Abel didn't answer.

"So, maybe I should introduce myself. I'm Mia. Most people know me by Chancellor Mia, but you can call me Mia." She tutted and shook her head. "You've been stirring up quite a bit of trouble, making my job very hard."

"You made your own job hard when you became a tyrant," Abel spat out.

Mia just laughed lightly, though it held no humor. "I know you've had struggles too. Losses. It's most unfortunate, the death of the young lady. What was her name? Harvey, Herriot? No matter," she said waving her hand. "She didn't have to die. And the lady at the newspaper, spouting all those lies."

Abel, for the first time in what felt like forever, felt energy surge through him and he lunged forward, hitting the end of his restraints. "Don't talk about Harley! You have no right! It's your fault she's dead and yours alone, you disrespectful scum of a human being!"

One of the guards took a step forward, but Mia held up her hand and they returned to their original position. "I have a deal for you—"

Abel didn't let her finish before spitting in her face. "I want no deal that you have to offer. I'd rather die than bend to your will."

Mia wiped under her eye where his saliva had landed and leaned forward. "Is that so?"

Abel didn't respond, but glared harder. Mia smirked and waved one of the guards over. "He says he would rather die. Do you want to help him with that Poppy?"

Poppy lifted her rifle and shoved the barrel in Abel's face. Abel stayed silent and stared Mia down. In no way would he ever beg for mercy. Mia pursed her lips and then smiled again. "I think you'll find my deal quite appealing. You tell me everything you know, everyone involved in this silly little rebellion, and I let you live a comfortable life here in my facility. Your mother is spared."

"If it's so silly, then why are you so worried about it?"

Poppy shoved her barrel a little closer to Abel's face so that it was actually touching his cheek now. Mia just smiled some more and said calmly. "It's just troublesome. Causes distrust, which means more work for me."

"So you've said," Abel muttered.

Mia was still placid with that stupid smile on her face. "You're being puerile. I'm offering you a long life with your mother. Security."

"At the loss of millions of others? This isn't about me."

"How selfless and noble," Mia praised. Abel clenched his jaw and ground his teeth. "And stupid."

Abel kept his mouth clamped shut, not trusting himself to say anything.

"I just want information. Where is Keturah hiding?" Abel kept his mouth shut. "Was it her who led the prison breakout?" Silence. "Fine. You obviously need a little...persuasion. Lucky for you, I have Kendra, a...persuasion expert."

Abel glared at Mia more and she shrugged. "Suit yourself. Kendra!" she screeched. "The usual starter. Get me when you're done. Ladies, let's leave Kendra to it. Poppy, Zia, guard the door."

Mia stood and everyone left except one woman. The woman gave Abel an evil grin. "I'm Kendra," she greeted in a happy enough voice.

Abel stayed silent and watched her out of the corner of his eye. She sat where Mia had previously been seated and slapped a large bag onto the table. She stood and walked around the table, kneeling down in front of Abel and tucking a strand of his overlong, messy black hair behind his ear. Abel jerked his head away and she pouted. "Fine. We'll do this the hard way then."

She opened up her bag and pulled out a knife. "How about we play a little game?"

Abel didn't answer.

"Here are the rules: for every question you don't answer you get a little cut. For every question you do answer, you get a reward. I have some bread over here. Ready? Where is Keturah?"

Abel stayed quiet. Kendra tutted and slowly dragged her knife across Abel's forearm. Pain seared up his entire arm as warm blood trickled from the cut. He refused to give her the satisfaction of letting out any noise of pain.

"What happened to the squad of males Chancellor Mia sent?"

He looked away from her and set his jaw. He felt hot pain sear up his other arm.

"Who is affiliated with you?"

Abel thought about Harley; her face filled his mind and suddenly the pain wasn't so bad. Kendra wasn't satisfied with his silence at all. She flicked her knife across Abel's face and scowled at him. "This game obviously isn't working. Should I escalate the difficulty?"

Abel stared at the wall in front of him and imagined Harley's laugh. He could practically hear her little snort. Despite the pain that enveloped him he found himself grinning. This seemed to frustrate Kendra further.

"Fine," she shrieked. "For every question you don't answer you lose a fingernail. How's that sound?"

Abel stared at his wall.

"Who's your mother, hmm?"

Abel didn't answer Kendra and she let out a small growl. She was holding a pair of clamp-like tweezers. She latched on to Abel's thumbnail and slowly began ripping it off. Abel wanted to cry out in pain, but he clinched his teeth together and scowled with determination. Kendra laughed lightly as Abel pressed his eyes shut with involuntary tears streaming down his cheeks, searing the slash on Abel's cheek. Maybe he should just tell her. Why should he have to suffer when it would be so easy to just give in, to tell her everything? He could live in peace away from the war and let someone else deal with it. Why did it have to be him?

He almost opened his mouth. He was so close to saying everything. It would all be over and Abel could live a long, happy life. The words were on the tip of his tongue. But then he reopened his eyes and saw the evil smirk on Kendra's face and he thought about everyone that would die if he told her anything, all the people that would suffer. And Mia was lying; there was no way that she'd let him live freely. Abel knew what had to be done; he bit his lip and stared Kendra straight in the eye.

"You'll give in eventually. They always do."

After an hour of interrogation, Abel had lost all the fingernails on his left hand, been slapped twice, and she even went as far as to whip his back. He refused to relent, though he had contemplated it in his moments of weakness, and Mia had returned.

"I see we've made progress," Mia said as she examined Abel.

Abel snorted despite the pain that coursed through his entire body.

"He's very resilient," Kendra reported.

Abel couldn't help but roll his eyes. Mia smirked. "Well, that's all for today I think. Clean his cuts and put him back in the chamber."

Abel sipped the water that was given to him.

Apparently cleaning wounds meant dumping a bottle of alcohol on them and calling it a day. One of the guards shoved him back into the chamber and closed the door. Abel couldn't lean against the wall because of the open wounds on his back. The stench was still present, so Abel knew that they hadn't bothered to wash it out.

He tried to sleep, but the pain was overwhelming, keeping him from even contemplating sleep. The noises and images filled his head again and he finally let out a hiss of pain now that he was alone. The hiss turned into a groan and then a whimper and a few tears slipped involuntarily from his eyes.

CHAPTER 46

Mia and the guards fetched Abel again in the morning, at least Abel assumed it was the morning. They went back to the same room and pushed Abel into the chair. His back pressed against the cold metal and he wanted to let out a scream of pain, but he bit his tongue. Poppy seemed satisfied with his reaction as she tied him down as tightly as possible.

"Give him a piece of bread," Mia ordered.

One of the guards came forward with a piece of bread and a glass of water. She pressed the glass to his lips and allowed him a sip before shoving the bread into his mouth. Mia smiled at Abel and leaned forward onto the table. "You've had all night to think and so have I. What's your conclusion?"

Abel glared at Mia. "I conclude that you will never win. You know why? Because in the end evil loses. Good wins. No matter how long it takes. I'm just a stepping stone, just a blade of grass in the giant picture. You can cut me down, but the truth will make it out eventually."

"See, that was my conclusion: no matter what I do to you, you won't bend and you won't break. But I think I've found a solution. Zia, go and grab X9562P."

Zia nodded, left the room, and reentered carrying a small bundle.

"Meet X9562P."

Zia held out the bundle for Abel to see. It was a baby! A sleeping, innocent baby! Abel's face softened slightly. Mia smirked when she noticed this. Zia set the baby on the table.

"See, I could torture you until you died and you wouldn't cave, but you'd never have someone else be harmed in your name. Maybe that's why the young woman's death affected you so much."

Abel caught on to what she was playing at. "You wouldn't," he breathed.

Mia's smirk grew and she raised her eyebrows. "You'd be surprised."

"I wouldn't," Abel growled. "You already kill babies anyway."

"So what's one more?" Mia said with a laugh. "Poppy, you heard the boy."

Poppy came forward and aimed her pistol at the baby's head. The baby opened its eyes, let out a long yawn, and when it saw Poppy, she began sobbing and screaming. Abel's eyes widened. They couldn't be serious!

"I'm not bluffing," Mia warned. "If you want to see this baby's head explode, fine by me. Poppy?"

Poppy cocked her pistol and simpered at Abel. "One..."

Abel sucked in a breath. He couldn't give in.

"Two..."

Abel narrowed his eyes with his mind racing to find a solution. There had to be one, right?

"Three..."

Abel watched in horror as Poppy began to pull the trigger. At the last second, Abel threw himself and the chair he was tied to into Poppy, sending her flying just as she pulled the trigger. A loud bang echoed around the room as Abel's chair and Abel rolled across the floor, jarring him and escalating his pain tenfold. But the baby was safe.

Someone jerked his chair upright and slammed it against the table, knocking the wind out of him and aggravating his whip marks.

For the first time, Mia's smile had slipped off of her face and she was scowling at Abel. "You're pushing too many boundaries, boy. My patience is wearing thin."

Poppy was glaring at Abel too and the baby had stopped crying.

"I don't push boundaries, I set them," Abel growled. "And I refuse to let you kill a baby and I refuse to give in to your whims. I. Will. Not. Allow it. I've been allowing of *you*, but that was obviously a mistake on my part."

Mia slapped Abel across the face and Abel spit blood at her. He had never been so consumed with hatred for someone in his entire life. "I change for no one or nothing and I will not give up. If you give up now, I'll be sparing with you."

"*You'll* be sparing with *me*? Listen hear, boy. You are in no position to be making threats."

"It isn't a threat, it's a promise," Abel seethed.

Mia narrowed her eyes at Abel. "Don't make promises you can't keep, boy."

"I haven't yet."

Mia growled, "Put him back in the chamber."

Poppy walked forward and untied Abel's feet from the chair and untied his arms, binding his hands together instead. Poppy turned away to grab something and Abel took his moment of opportunity. He swung his knee up, nailing Poppy in the face and knocking her to the side. She moaned from the ground and Abel surged forward towards the door. Zia tried to step in front of him, but Abel remembered William.

You have a hard head, dude.

Abel barreled forward, not slowing down and ducked his head at the last second, slamming into the woman trying to block his path. He seemed to have surprised them, but he was sure the shock would wear off soon, so Abel had to get out of there quickly before someone drew a weapon.

A woman dove forward and grabbed his ankle, but Abel kicked her in the face and she released, grabbing her face and crying out.

Abel ran to the door, and opened it as quickly as he could with his hands bound. He slammed it closed behind himself and locked everyone in to buy himself some time. The hallway was empty and everything was bright white. Abel jogged down the hall and took a left, trying to put as much distance as possible between him and the room full of angry women. He hooked another left and heard alarms begin to blare. He kept running even though he didn't know where he was going.

Abel heard footsteps behind him and ducked into a room that was to his right. He shut the door quietly and examined where he was. It was some sort of closet filled with the guards' uniforms. And then an idea hit Abel. He looked around for something to cut his binds. In the back corner there was a supply of weapons. Abel grinned and went over to the knives, maneuvering so that it cut the ropes that tied him.

He shed his issued cotton clothes and pulled on the biggest uniform they had. Apparently they had some pretty big women in the guard force because it all fit Abel, even the shoes. The shirt burned against his back from the open wounds, but Abel endured it. He pulled a helmet over his head and grabbed a few weapons: a pistol, two knives, and a rifle strapped to his back. He poked his head out to see if anyone was coming. When he saw no one, Abel stepped out into the hallway and began marching.

He didn't encounter anyone for the first few hallways that he walked down. He thought that might be able to get away without any trouble, so that, of course, was when trouble came.

Abel was trying to find an exit when he heard the synchronized pounding of footsteps.

"Hey! You there!"

Abel winced and turned around.

"Where's your squad?" the women in front of the organized group demanded.

"The boy attacked me. I got separated from my group, so I was trying to track him," Abel responded, trying to make his voice as girly as possible.

The woman nodded. "Who's your squad leader?"

Abel tried to think of a name that he knew was a part of the guards. "Poppy."

"What's your guard ID number?"

Shit. Abel knew that he couldn't fake this. He assessed how many women there were. There was no way that he could fight through them all.

"I'm new," Abel excused. "I haven't quite memorized it yet."

The woman looked skeptical but didn't say anything. "We were just going on our routine patrol around the outside of the building."

Abel's heart soared. Maybe he would be fine after all. "Could I join your patrol unit until Poppy contacts me?"

The woman was silent for a few moments and then nodded. "That is protocol: if you get separated from your team and encounter another one, join them."

What dumb luck!

Abel got in line next to a woman at the end and they continued marching. When they got outside, Abel tried to assess his surroundings and figure out where he was. Surrounding the building that he had just exited was a large concrete wall, and just beyond that Abel could make out the tops of trees. Maybe he wasn't as far away from Keturah's hideout as he had suspected.

Abel began to lag behind the group of guards gradually so they wouldn't notice. He looked for some point of weakness in the wall where he could get over, under, around, or through. They rounded a corner and a gate came into view. A gate that he could hop....

He looked around. No one was here except for the squad he had tagged along with. Abel broke into a sprint, drawing the attention of the guards he had been with. "Stop!"

Abel kept running at top speed. At the fence, he lifted his legs as high off the ground as physically possible and used his hand to swing himself over. He heard gunfire from behind him, but he didn't look back; he just kept running into the forest. He heard shouting behind him and heavy footfalls, but Abel didn't dare turn around. He just kept running for as long as his legs would carry him.

CHAPTER 47

Two weeks had come and gone since they had received the note. Justin knew that if they were going to kill Abel, today would be the day. A dreary mood settled over everyone. They all knew. They could feel it in the air. Justin tried to cheer up the guys by playing cards with them, but it only made them think of Abel more and Jesse actually started crying. Peter hadn't spoken a word since Abel had been kidnapped.

Abel had sacrificed his life for them, for their cause. Justin slumped down in his chair by the fire, but then shook his head and stood. He had to be the good example for the boys. He had to be their source of comfort, their bravery.

Justin tried to force a smile onto his face, but it came out more as a grimace. He walked into the circular room where all the other boys were congregated, sitting silently and staring off into space. Justin cleared his throat and the boys glanced over at him. "Has Sarah stopped by?" he asked.

Lee shook his head and placed it in his hands. "I think Keturah's going to bring us breakfast."

Justin nodded. Silence ensued again and Justin pressed his eyes closed. He didn't know how to cheer *himself* up let alone the ten other boys that were relying on him.

Sarah and other spies within the government had been trying to get information on Abel's situation, but it was highly classified. Only Chancellor Mia and a select few people even *knew* that Abel was being held prisoner. Supposedly there was a whole other facility that was hidden and that no one knew about where they were holding Abel.

To everyone's surprise, Sarah waltzed in carrying their breakfast. She smiled at them and Justin's jaw nearly dropped. "Morning, boys," she greeted with a warm smile.

All of the guys' heads shot up and they raised their eyebrows. "M-morning," Justin spluttered.

Sarah laughed at their befuddled expressions. But Justin heard a little crack at the end. She was trying to be strong for them, just as Justin had been attempting and failing to do.

"I brought breakfast," she said softly.

The boys nodded silently. "So what are your plans for today?" Sarah prompted.

Justin decided this was his cue. He snorted. "What are our plans for any day?"

Sarah gave him an appreciative smile and some of the other boys cracked a smile. "I was thinking that I'd hang out here today. I don't get to spend much time with you guys."

And so they did. And not once did Justin catch Sarah's grin falter and soon the boys were smiling too. And momentarily, the boys forgot that Abel had been sentenced to death today. And momentarily they were happy. Justin could tell that Sarah was breaking, and he didn't know how to help.

CHAPTER 48

Abel had been walking for about a week. He had found the river in the woods, but apparently it was a lot longer than he had first thought it to be. He also didn't know which direction to follow it. Based on the sun that rose in the east and set in the west, the river ran from north to south. He was pretty sure that Keturah's bunker was northern-ish.

He walked continually, day and night, until he couldn't move at all anymore. Then he'd collapse by the river and allow himself a drink of water to sustain his energy. He hadn't had any food since the slice of bread at the compound where they had been holding him. Abel was dead on his feet, but he kept moving despite his body's protest. After about the tenth day of walking, when Abel was sure he wouldn't be able to move another step, he saw the sky scraper that he knew as the capitol building. His body that had previously been protesting to stop surged with a newfound energy. He pressed forward at a pace he hadn't moved at since his great escape.

His feet pounded through the forest as he tried to not trip on branches and roots. Just a little further, he told himself. Abel then saw something else he recognized: the clearing. Abel felt like shouting for joy, but his voice didn't work anyways. He galloped forward and searched for the secret staircase in the foliage. Words couldn't describe how he felt as he pulled open the trapdoor and descended the beautiful, perfect, amazing staircase. The long hallway was a welcoming embrace and finally the circular room revealed itself.

Abel pulled open the door and was met by the shocked faces of the boys. They all stood still for a moment and then Peter leaped up and tackled Abel into a hug. Justin followed and then Lee and Austin and Jesse and William and Gabe and Quincy and Matthew, Isaiah, and Garrett even joined in until Abel was on the ground and they were dog-piled on top of him. Abel didn't have enough energy to speak. Eventually all the boys got off and Justin pulled Abel up and hugged him again. Justin's shoulders were shaking slightly and Abel realized that he was crying. Abel tried to wrap his arms around Justin, but he ended up collapsing in his arms. He wasn't able to support his own weight.

Justin wrapped his arm under Abel and helped him to a chair. "Water," Abel muttered.

Justin looked at the other boys. "Do we have any water?"

"I have a water bottle from when Sarah last came," Peter offered.

Justin motioned him forward and Peter handed him the water. Justin carefully tipped it to Abel's lips and allowed him a quick sip. Abel swallowed slowly and allowed the cool liquid to soothe his scratchy throat.

"Do we have any food?" Abel choked out.

Justin looked at the boys. "I have some fruit," Austin spoke up.

He came forward and began feeding Abel the raspberries. Abel chewed slowly, letting his stomach adjust to the sudden sustenance. He felt the effects of the sugar in the fruit almost immediately. Abel opened his mouth and allowed Austin to put another raspberry into it. He once again chewed slowly, savoring the tart juice and letting it slide down his throat at a leisurely pace.

Abel could only eat about ten raspberries before his stomach groaned in protest and he felt completely full. But he finally felt like he could talk. No one pressured him to speak. Everyone could sense that Abel had been through a traumatic experience. Abel's pain hadn't decreased much over the past week. He was sure that his whip marks were still apparent and maybe even infected. His nails had just started to grow back, his bruises had just begun to lighten, and his cuts from Kendra's knives had scabbed over.

Abel pulled off his shirt that was rubbing against his back uncomfortably and he heard a few gasps as his whip marks were revealed. He pressed his eyes together and let out a hiss of pain.

"We need to wash those," Peter said in a soft whisper.

Abel reopened his eyes and saw everyone staring at him. He sighed and closed his eyes again. He just wanted everything to stop: the pain, the suffering, the stares, the exhaustion, the weariness, the fear. Abel opened his eyes and watched as Peter exited into the bathroom and returned with a towel, a bowl of water, soap, and a sheet.

Peter began dabbing water on the open wounds and Abel hissed in pain every time Peter touched him.

After Peter had gotten most of the blood and pus and whatnot off, he began to clean the wounds with the soap which caused Abel to moan and groan in pain even more. Then Peter wrapped the wounds with strips of the sheet and helped Abel into bed. Abel let his eyes slide shut and he tried to forget the echoes of torture that was ringing in his ears. He fell asleep not long after, giving in to his body, begging for rest.

CHAPTER 49

When Abel reopened his eyes, Sarah was next to him, holding his hand and crying. "Mom?" he croaked.

"Abel," she whispered. "Oh, baby. It's okay, I have you now."

"I love you," he murmured.

Abel's mom smiled through her tears and nodded. "I love you, too, baby." She brought Abel's hand to her lips, kissing it gently.

Abel licked his lips. "Water?" he asked.

His mother smiled and handed him a glass with water inside. Abel sipped it gradually and allowed his mother to feed him some breakfast that she had with her. He could only get down a couple of bites before his stomach protested and he felt nauseous.

Abel felt filthy (mostly because he was). Dirt coated his body, mixing with urine and feces and blood. His hair was matted to his head and he smelled revolting. He wanted nothing more than a nice, hot shower, but he knew that it would hurt unbelievably on his back. And he wasn't sure that he had the strength to stand. Abel sighed and took another small sip of the water.

"Where are the boys?" he asked.

"They left to give you some privacy," his mom explained.

Abel nodded and fell silent again. He didn't know what to say anymore. He didn't want to talk about the torture and he didn't want to talk about the escape. He felt sort of distanced from everyone else. His mom let a frown slip onto her lips as Abel began to stare off into the distance, trying to forget, trying to remember.

"I'll go get them," Sarah offered.

Abel just nodded, still staring off into space. Abel's mom stood and left the room, returning with Keturah and the boys.

Keturah sat at the end of Abel's bed and gave him a sad smile. "Hey, Abel," she said gently.

Abel turned his head to look at her. "How are you feeling?"

Abel shrugged. "Fine, I guess."

Keturah exchanged looks with Sarah. Abel knew that they were concerned by his lack of...everything. He attempted a smile to prove his point, but it probably looked more like a grimace. "Can I take a shower?" he asked.

"That probably isn't good for your back," Peter informed him.

"Neither is being soaked in urine, feces, blood, and dirt," Abel replied. Peter clamped his mouth shut; Abel could tell he had been a little harsh and that the boys were shocked to hear that he had been sitting in his own pee.

"What's wrong with his back?" Keturah asked.

So the guys hadn't told her anything. Abel sat up and turned around to show Keturah and his mom the whip marks. Sarah gasped and Keturah tutted like she knew this would happen but had hoped otherwise.

"It's going to hurt," Peter warned, "but I don't see why you can't take a shower."

"It already hurts; I'm sure that it won't be much worse," Abel grunted, trying to ignore the searing pain that burned through his whole body.

Abel was wrong. The hot water hitting the open wounds hurt *so* much more. He was as quick as humanly possible in the shower and then he hopped, towel drying everything except his back and throwing on a clean pair of pants, but leaving the shirt off. He walked back into the bedroom and collapsed onto his bed, his energy completely expended. His mom handed him some water and Abel sipped it gingerly.

Keturah cleared her throat. "I know you probably don't want to talk about what happened, but I'm going to need you to tell me."

Abel sighed. He had figured that this was coming. "Where do I start?"

"I know what happened here, but I need to know what happened after they took you."

"When I woke up, I was in a tiny room. It was barely big enough for me to lie down in. It was so dark that I couldn't tell the difference between my eyes being open and them being closed. And it was freezing. I had been changed out of my clothes and into plain cotton shorts and a shirt." He looked up from his lap to see everyone listening with rapt attention. He cleared his throat and took another sip of water before continuing. "After a while they began messing with my brain, reaching into my deepest subconscious and extracting my fears, making me live them over and over."

"The chamber of fear," Sarah whispered.

Abel nodded. "The chamber of fear. After I had grown used to the cold and dark, they switched it to unbearably bright and sweltering hot. Then, they took me to an interrogation room, they gave me a glass of water, and Mia tried to cut me a deal: tell her everything and Mom and I would get to live in peace for the rest of our lives."

"Lies," Keturah hissed.

Abel nodded again. "I refused to tell her anything, so she called in her torture specialist. That's where I got these," Abel said motioning to his back, the cuts on his arms, the bruises, and the fingernails. "I still didn't tell them anything. They threw me back into the chamber and the next morning, they let me out again, gave me another glass of water and a slice of bread, and Mia told me that she knew how to get to me; she tried to shoot a baby in the head in front of me unless I told her everything. I took my opportunity, knocked into the shooter and escaped. I had to hike through the woods for over a week until I got here."

Abel looked up again and saw everyone staring at him in awe. "You—you went through all of that and you didn't tell them *anything*?" Justin inquired sounding in awe.

Abel squirmed a little under all of their gazes. "Well, yeah."

Justin slowly broke into a grin and began clapping and the other boys soon followed suit. Keturah looked proud as did his mother. "Do we have any more food?" Abel asked.

Sarah shook her head and laughed, handing Abel some breakfast.

CHAPTER 50

Over the next couple of days, the boys hardly left Abel's side as though they were afraid that if they did, he'd disappear. Abel was not unhappy for the company. They helped Sarah sew new clothes for everyone. Justin kept stabbing himself with the needle and letting out a string of cuss words. "How do you do this?" he exclaimed, throwing down the cloth that he had been trying to make a shirt out of. Though, it looked more like a deformed poodle.

Sarah laughed. "I've been doing this for a long time. They don't exactly sell male clothes anymore."

Peter, it turns out, was an expert at sewing. He had already managed to make three pairs of pants, five shirts, and a few jackets. "It isn't that hard," he protested.

Justin shoved him, making him stab his thumb and drop the shorts that he had been working on. "Ow," Peter said, shooting Justin a glare as all the other boys laughed.

"At least you can get the thread onto the needle," Lee whined. He had been trying in vain to thread the needle since they had started. His tongue was poking out of his mouth and his face was scrunched in concentration.

"Oh, stop complaining," Isaiah scolded. "It's less work for you." Isaiah was okay at sewing as far as Abel could tell, but he absolutely despised it.

Abel laughed at the boys' shenanigans. They had been exaggeratedly silly since he got back and Abel could tell they were all trying to make him feel better.

Jesse tossed aside the shirt he had just finished. "It's not so bad," he admitted. "It's just time consuming."

"Luckily we have lots of time to consume," Austin pointed out.

Jesse shrugged as he rethreaded his needle.

"When's lunch?" Austin asked.

Abel rolled his eyes. "We just ate breakfast."

"That was *forever* ago," Austin whined.

Garrett scoffed. "That was like two hours ago."

"My point exactly," Austin said as if it were super obvious.

Gabriel, who was ever silent, just rolled his eyes and glanced over at his brother, William. William shook his head at Gabriel; they seemed very efficient at their nonverbal communication. Gabriel shrugged and refocused on his sewing and William smirked.

"Are we done yet?" Matthew asked. From anyone else it would've sounded whiny, but Matthew had a knack for taking something that would usually sound negative and making it sound positive.

"Almost," Sarah promised.

"Thank God," Isaiah sighed in relief.

Jesse rolled his eyes, but didn't comment. Abel had noticed that ever since he got back, the boys seemed to be getting along better. Matthew and Garrett didn't fight as much and neither did Isaiah and Jesse. Abel was glad that they had somewhat settled their differences, but sometimes he still felt a pang of jealousy.

They all were like one large family; they got on so well and they even fought, but at the end of the day they were all brothers. Abel wanted that so badly, but he was afraid that it would never be the same between him and the guys for multiple reasons. They looked up to him way too much. Abel didn't deserve the kind of treatment they gave him, like he was some kind of hero. And they were so bonded; Abel hadn't known them for as long as they had known each other and he hadn't been through what they went through with them. Abel was jealous because he so often felt left out even though he was a part of whatever was going on, even though they were his friends.

He watched as they laughed and talked together and sighed, wishing that he could be a part of it. But then he mentally slapped himself. Of course he could be a part of it! All he had to do was join in the conversation. Abel opened his mouth to say something, but he was cut off by Garrett.

"I finally finished!"

Abel held back a scowl and cleared his throat. But then he didn't know what to say. That was the most awful feeling, wanting so badly to talk to them, but having absolutely nothing to say.

"So Abel, I heard that you used to put a sheet over your head and try to escape your room," Justin joked.

Abel chuckled. "I looked so stupid. I can't believe I actually thought that would work. You told them about that?"

"Oh yeah! I've told them all of your embarrassing stories," Sarah said. "But you finally found something that did hide you so you could sneak out," she muttered.

Abel gave her a sheepish grin. Justin laughed and said, "Well, one good thing came of it."

"And what would that be?" Abel wondered.

"Everything that's happened since."

"Does that count as one thing?" Quincy interjected.

"Way to ruin the moment," Peter said under his breath.

Abel laughed and shook his head. The momentary feeling of envy had passed and he became absorbed in the retelling of the time Austin decided it would be a great prank to switch everyone's helmets so none of them fit the guards during their one hour of freedom. By the time he was done telling the tale, Peter had already made three more shirts and it was lunch time.

"I'll get Austin's first since he's so impatient," Sarah teased.

Abel's mom had explained to him the method she had to get food as to not draw suspicion. She would have one person from the rebellion deliver food to a specific, predetermined spot where Sarah would pick it up and bring it back to the bunker. She repeated this until everyone had food. It was a long process now that there were twelve men to feed not to mention the people that were in hiding at Keturah's other underground hideouts. Abel was pretty sure that his mom didn't have to deliver food to them though.

By the time that Sarah had gotten everyone's food and returned, Abel's back had begun to sear with pain again. Peter had been taking good care of him and his mom managed to smuggle him some pain pills due to his constant throbbing fingers, burning back, and uncomfortable bruises.

Abel found himself unable to pay attention to anything or eat any of the food he had been given due to the pain. He pressed his eyes closed and let out a low, unintentional moan, drawing the attention of everyone.

"His meds must be wearing off," Peter analyzed.

"Why doesn't he say anything?" Sarah tutted.

"It's a guy thing," Justin supplemented.

"It's stupid," Sarah argued.

"It's pride; men want to be independent, we don't want to admit that we need help...even if we do," Justin explained.

"So men are prideful and stubborn?" Sarah summed up.

"Pretty much," Lee agreed, "but you didn't hear it from me."

"Grab him a pill, Peter," Justin said.

It was silent for a moment and then Abel felt a hand on his shoulder. He opened his eyes and saw Peter offering him a pill and a glass of water. Abel frowned, sighed, and grudgingly accepted the pill; he hated taking them. They made him sleepy and groggy and less aware.

Abel waited a few minutes for the medicine to kick in and then began to eat as the nausea from the pain subsided. When he had finished eating, everyone was already done and had resumed their sewing, talking amongst themselves. "This is everyone's last one," Sarah announced.

"Finally," Isaiah hissed.

Jesse smirked. "You could always do extra if you want, Isaiah. You sound so sad to be finished."

Isaiah gave Jesse a flat look and continued sewing.

"God bless it!" Justin exclaimed as he stabbed himself for the millionth time.

"Wimp," Garrett teased. "Look at Abel. Do you see him complaining about hurting?"

Justin blushed and stared intently at his sewing.

"Isn't that always how it is though?" Abel offered, trying to make Justin feel better. "We complain about the little things, but don't say anything about the things that really matter, really hurt."

Justin smiled at Abel and Abel knew he had said the right thing. A warmth spread through his chest and he returned Justin's grin. Then his eyes began to droop and he knew the meds had fully kicked in, pulling him into a deep sleep.

CHAPTER 51

Abel decided that he wanted to see the poorer parts of Femater. He knew what Harley had told him about it: most people lived in slum-like neighborhoods and a vast percentage was actually homeless. But he actually wanted to see how bad it was. When he went on adventures with Harley, they tended to stay in the middle to upper class areas. He wanted to get a grasp of the disparity between people like Chancellor Mia and people like that Marge lady that had "flipped Abel off" at the diner.

When his mother came to give Abel and the boys breakfast, Abel told her his idea.

"I can't today, Abel. I have things to do."

"Well, that's okay. I kind of wanted to do it by myself anyways," Abel explained.

He knew he was pushing his luck, but he just felt that this was something that he needed to do by himself.

Sarah gave Abel an incredulous look. "No," she shot down.

"I have the HSD. And I'll be extra careful," Abel promised.

Sarah raised an eyebrow at Abel and narrowed her eyes.

"Besides, it's not like any government officials will be there," Abel pointed out.

Sarah sighed. "There's no way I can stop you, is there?"

"No, this was more of a formality," Abel agreed.

Sarah let out another sigh and glared at her son. "Fine."

Abel grinned. "I'll be back before supper."

"You're going to be the death of me," his mom muttered under her breath.

Abel quickly ate his breakfast and grabbed the HSD, bidding the boys and his mother goodbye. He faltered for a moment at the stairs, remembering what happened when he got caught. Maybe he should take someone with him.

He shook his head. What good would it be to get two people captured instead of one? *If* he got caught. He continued upstairs and opened the trapdoor, closing it carefully and turning off the force field that Keturah had installed as another protective measure. After leaving its vicinity, he reactivated it and the rest of the security systems. He continued through the forest, listening to the random noises and the crunch of leaves beneath his feet.

He got back to the main road fairly easily, managing not to get turned around (which happened often because after a while in the forest, everything looked the same). He followed the road for a bit, taking turns onto the roads that looked especially worn and cracked. Abel didn't particularly know where he was going, but he figured that if he followed the poorer looking roads and neighborhoods, he'd eventually get to where he was going. It couldn't be that hard.

He finally got to a road that just made Abel want to puke. The stench was awful and it was dreary and tattered. Houses lined the street, but most had boarded up windows, broken glass, graffiti, decaying structures, and rats scurrying around. Families sat on the sides of the roads, leaning against each other and huddling for warmth. Their clothes were in shreds with dirt encasing the fabric. Most of them didn't have shoes on and most of them looked sick. They all looked tired and depressed. They barely moved when Abel walked by except to lift their heads and glare at him. It was nearly silent except for the occasional cough. All of them looked deathly pale and painfully thin. Abel had lost weight during his two to three weeks without much food, but it was nothing compared to these families.

Abel stopped in the middle of the road and stared at his surroundings; it was so miserable, so sick. All the people looked like stray dogs that had given hope long ago. He took a few more steps and jumped as he stepped in a suspiciously sludge-like puddle, breaking the previous silence.

Abel noticed that there were very few children. He remembered something Harley had told him.

The government just evicted her and repossessed her children.

Abel, being wiser to the government now, knew that "repossessing" probably lead to murdering. He stared in shock at the scene; it was worse than he had expected. *Way* worse. An elderly lady in front of Abel raised a crooked finger and curled it for Abel to go over to her.

He hesitantly made his way over and crouched next to her. "What are you doing here, girl?"

Girl? What did she mean? Then Abel remembered that he had the HSD on. "I-I wanted to see...."

"See what?"

"What it was like. How bad it was."

The old lady let out a cackle. "Well, have a good look, girl. This is what it's like. Rich people like you—" She was cut off by her own rasping cough. "Rich people like you," she continued after getting her hacking under control, "don't care about people like me."

Abel shook his head. "That isn't true. I care and I know plenty of people who care."

The woman laughed again. It was mirthless and cold. "You don't care. You came to gawk at me. What have you done to make a difference?"

He stayed silent. Abel couldn't tell her what he'd done, what he was *doing*. She mistook his silence for confirmation. "Exactly. You wanted to come gawk at me to make yourself feel like you were doing something, to ease your conscience."

Abel stayed silent again and the old lady submitted to another bout of coughs that racked through her entire body. "Careful, Rich Girl, you might catch my diseases." She sounded so cynical and mocking. "Looking at me makes you sick; I can see it in your eyes."

Abel shook his head again. "Not looking at you, looking at what you were forced to endure. Looking at you makes me sad and angry and hopeful and driven."

"Hopeful? Driven? You are messed up, Rich Girl."

Abel just shook his head again and stood to leave. He couldn't bear being there anymore. It was horrible and cruel and sickening. He made his way back to the bunker. When he got back the guys asked him about what he saw, but Abel just shook his head and refused to talk about it. He couldn't relay the tale, or what it made him feel..

CHAPTER 52

The next Monday came and the meeting was underway. Ketruah was having everyone do their normal reports when Hillary stood and said, "Our numbers have over tripled. We should lead the attack on the capitol building this Friday. It's a holiday, Male Eradication Day, so there'll be limited staff."

Keturah looked to Sarah. "It's true," Sarah confirmed.

Keturah nodded. "I just completed the plans for the invasion, too. Let's review..."

And so Keturah went over their strategy, who she wanted present, their plan of attack, how they were going to take control of the building, and whatnot. When she had finished explaining, Keturah adjourned the meeting and everyone slowly filtered out, leaving Abel, the boys and Keturah.

Keturah walked over to Abel and said, "We're having a second meeting later today."

"What? Why?"

Keturah smiled mischievously. "I accidentally left out some details to the plan of attack."

Abel tilted his head, but Keturah didn't say anymore and left down the hallway. Abel shook his head and shrugged. "I need to change your bandages," Peter said to Abel.

"Okay. Be gentler this time."

Peter laughed. "You say that every time."

"That's because it hurts every time," Abel quipped.

Peter rolled his eyes and led Abel into the bathroom, undoing Abel's bandages and washing the wounds. "It's looking better."

"Well, it isn't feeling better," Abel hissed as Peter began washing the gashes.

Peter chuckled lightly and rewrapped the bandages. "Let's go see if Justin has any painkillers left."

Peter walked into the bedroom and Abel followed him. Justin was playing a game of cards with Garrett and Lee. The other boys were talking about something on Austin's bed.

"Do you have any painkillers left?" Peter asked Justin. "Abel's back is bugging him."

Abel snorted. Bugging was a little bit of an understatement. "Sure," Justin replied setting his cards down and turning his back to grab a bottle off of his nightstand. While his back was turned Lee picked up his cards and peeked quickly before setting them back down as Justin turned back around.

Abel tried to repress his laughter, but Justin noticed. "What?" he queried.

"Nothing," Abel denied. Justin rolled his eyes and handed Abel the bottle with a few pills in it.

As Abel walked away he could faintly here the beginnings of an argument. "Hey!" Justin exclaimed. Lee responded but Abel couldn't hear. He laughed to himself and swallowed one of the pills. Abel went and sat on his own bed, picking up Harley's journal and flipping through the pages. He could almost imagine her writing in it. He read a few more pages before he heard Keturah come back in. Soon after, everyone else filed into the meeting room and sat down.

"So with the battle plan, I forgot a little detail. It's going to be exactly like I said except...."

Abel grinned as Keturah went on. He completely agreed and he could tell that most everyone in the audience did too. It was perfect. Now Abel was sure that they'd succeed on Friday. Positive.

CHAPTER 53

Mia walked down the empty hallway with her heels clicking and echoing and reverberating against the tall ceilings. She had to do something. She had to stop the revolutionists; it was already getting out of hand. Five riots just in the past week. Mia rubbed her eyes. She hadn't slept for three days. Everybody was already petitioning for impeachment.

She entered the meeting room and walked to the front, straightening the papers in her hands. Mia cleared her throat, gaining the attention of everybody in the room.

"Previously this week I did a press release to try and ease the tension and unrest of the people. Obviously it did not work as well as I would have hoped. The new plan of action is as follows: if anyone who talks about revolting, if anyone who riots, if anyone who even implies that they are minutely sympathetic towards Keturah, arrest them. If they resist, shoot them."

"What about the escaped boy? Are we going after him?" Poppy asked. "And the male squad we had, what about them?"

"No," Mia said harsher than she had meant to. Poppy didn't seem surprised by her tone though.

Mia pressed her eyes shut and sighed. "We need not worry about them. They will be dealt with soon enough."

No one questioned Mia. They all seemed to realize how close she was to snapping. She glared at them all. "If even one slips past you and word gets back to me about it, it'll be one week in the chamber for you and then extermination. Do not fail me," she barked, sending one final glare to all the guards and then departing back to her office. So much work to do and so little time. She had to prepare for her plan. Everything had to be perfect.

CHAPTER 54

Friday came faster than Abel had expected it would, but he was ready. Keturah rallied the troops, prepared the supplies, and led the way to the capitol building. When they finally got there, Keturah led to the sewer entrance that Hillary had suggested. She ushered them in in the order they had discussed, Abel being in front. The first thing that hit him was the stench. There was murky water circling his feet that he didn't want to think about. He let his eyes adjust and then began trudging through the slush that had seeped into his shoes and went up to his knees. The sewer tunnel was circular and Abel had to duck his head in order to fit in it.

He could hear people splashing along behind him, but he kept his eyes trained forward, following the long, windy path and trying not to slip. After about twenty minutes of marching he saw the access panel that Hillary had told them about. He held up his hand for everyone behind him to stop; there were only about fifty people in his strike team. Keturah made her way to the front and whispered, "This is it. This is what we've been preparing for. Let's go."

She opened the access door and let Abel step out first. He heard people getting out behind him, but his eyes were trained in front of him. Blocking the hallway was a small army with Hillary and Mia standing in front with smirks on their faces. It was a trap.

CHAPTER 55

Abel let out a small gasp and said, "Hillary?"

Hillary let out an almost maniacal laugh. "Yes. I tricked you all."

"But why?" Abel wondered. "Why would you do this to us?"

"Did you really think that I had changed?" She laughed again. "No. I never changed. I was feeding you false information and spying for Mia. I'm the one who told the location of the bunker. Why do you think no one was worried when the male squad went missing? Why do you think we didn't send someone to recapture you after you escaped?"

"Why?" Abel asked shaking his head.

"You really think that I blame myself for Harley's death? No. That was all you, Abel. You poisoned her mind, led her astray. Had it not been for you, Harley would be happily following in my footsteps."

"You're delusional," Abel spat. "Harley hated you. She would never have followed in your anything."

Abel could see that Hillary wanted to scoff. Harley's mom, who Abel had learned was named Holly, stepped forward and glared at Hillary, saying, "I am so disappointed in you, Hillary. I raised you better than this."

"You never raised me, *Mom*. I raised myself! You were always too busy with the rebellion and then you were too busy with precious Harley. You never loved me and you certainly never raised me. That was where Mia came in, picking up the slack that you were so happy to drop."

"That's not true and you know it!" Holly protested.

Abel checked the time on his watch. Almost.

He glared at Hillary and said, "Nonetheless, we're obviously caught now. What're you going to do with us, with the other rebels? This is only a tiny fraction of our sympathizers."

"You all will be tortured for information and then disposed of. As for your other sympathizers, they will all be tracked down and either persuaded to the correct beliefs or disposed of as well. Or maybe we'll just implant the BWS and make our own personal army," Mia mused. "Either way, it's game over."

A loud explosion echoed across the entire building and the floor shook. Footsteps echoed down the hall and Sarah laughed from behind Mia with a gun pointed to her head. "You bet it is."

CHAPTER 56

Mia's face morphed from triumph to shock. "Wh-what?" she spluttered.

Sarah smirked. "You see, Keturah and the rest of us are pretty smart; we knew Hillary was faking, so we let her think she was winning. Abel and Keturah were to lead an 'attack' through the suggested entrance and distract you while I led a different attack on the opposite end of the building, taking out your main systems and projecting your darkest secrets over the security systems in every building, every house, every street light. How's that for game over?"

Abel, Keturah, the boys, and everyone else had also pulled out their weapons and pointed them at the blockade in front of them. "Surrender now and you will get a fair trial," Abel barked.

A few people set their weapons on the ground and held their hands in the air. Abel motioned for Holly and the others to tie those people up. Others from Mia's army stood their ground, digging in their heels and glancing hesitantly at Mia and Sarah.

"Make one wrong move and we open fire," Abel warned.

A few others set their weapons down and allowed themselves to be tied up. There were less than twenty people that were still standing their ground including Hillary and Mia. Abel took a step forward and repeated, "We will give you a fair trial if you surrender. If we feel threatened in any way, we will open fire."

Lightning fast, Hillary shoved her hand into her pocket and pulled out a gun, shooting Abel with a loud bang. Chaos ensued as the others began shooting and Abel fell to the ground.

CHAPTER 57

Abel couldn't move as shots rang out around him. Everything seemed faraway and in slow motion. He pressed a hand to his shoulder where the bullet had hit. He couldn't allow himself to black out. He applied as much pressure as possible. Finally, the gunshots stopped and Justin and Gabriel hovered over him. "He needs medical attention. More than we can provide," Justin admitted.

"Do you think a hospital would accept him now?" Gabriel wondered.

"Maybe," Justin conceded.

"I don't see why not," William said.

"Here," Garrett offered, taking off his shirt and ripping it in two. "Stuff this into the bullet hole."

Matthew took it out of Garrett's hand and gingerly stuffed it into the front hole. "I'm going to sit you up now," he warned Abel.

Abel couldn't speak let alone move, so he just allowed Matthew to push him up into a sitting position. Pain seared up his entire side. Matthew motioned for Garrett to put the other half of his shirt in the exit wound. Abel couldn't think at all as the pain consumed him. His mom walked forward. "Keturah said to go ahead and escort him to the hospital and to detain anyone who gives us grief."

Justin nodded and said, "Garrett you support left, Matt you support right. If he passes out, get Isaiah and Jesse to grab his legs."

They pulled Abel up and supported most of his weight as he attempted to shuffle his feet. They got back out through the front entrance an Abel managed to keep his eyes open for the next few roads, but the pain overwhelmed him and he ended up passing out.

CHAPTER 58

When Abel opened his eyes, everything was white and a beeping filled the room, echoing off the walls in the silence. Abel surveyed his surroundings; he was in a hospital.

The door opened and in came a lady wearing a white lab coat and carrying a HoloNet. Behind her were Abel's mom and Justin and Keturah. "You're awake!" Sarah cheered.

"You are so lucky, dude," Justin grinned.

Keturah just shook her head and said, "I'll let the doctor explain."

The lady smiled at Abel and said, "I just wanted you to know that I was always a supporter, just silently. Anyway, the bullet traveled less the half an inch away from one of your main arteries to you heart. I was able to repair the damage and you should heal perfectly fine. You'll be released within four days. I'll leave you to talk with your family. Press that button if you need anything."

She smiled one last time and left Abel with his mom, Keturah and Justin. "Family?" he echoed.

"We had to lie to be able to see you," Justin explained. "Well, except for your mom; she really is your family."

"Now what?" Abel wondered aloud.

Keturah shrugged. "We'll make it up as we go. That's what I've been doing this entire time anyway."

They all laughed and talked and everything felt right for the first time in a very long time. It wasn't perfect, nor would it probably ever be, but it was well on its way and Abel was content.

Later that day, Austin, Lee, Jesse, Isaiah, Garrett, William, Quincy, Peter, Gabriel, and Matthew somehow managed to sneak in. Abel didn't ask and he was sure that he didn't want to know. They brought cards and food and said that Abel couldn't miss out on the celebratory feast. Sarah and Keturah had left already, making it only the boys.

"To the first of many victories," Justin toasted.

"Here, here," the boys agreed.

"To the first of many," Abel echoed.

Abel wondered *how* many. When would it be over? But then a realization smacked him in the face with the force of a brick wall: it would never be over. Because as long as there was a differing of opinion, no matter whether the battle, or even the war, was over, people would fight for what they believe in. Corruption would eventually worm it's way into whatever solution they found because no one and nothing was perfect.

EPILOGUE

3 years later....

Sarah's HoloNet buzzed in her pocket and she removed it and pressed the answer button. A miniature hologram appeared in Sarah's palm and the doctor began speaking. "I have good news..."

Sarah hung up after the conversation and hurried straight home to tell Abel.

Abel listened to all his mother had to say incredulously. It couldn't be true. It had been so long and yet, it felt like yesterday. "Can we go right now?" he asked excitedly.

His mom laughed. "Yes."

She led the way to the private hospital room that she had mentioned earlier. Holly was already inside and the doctor was talking to her as tears streamed down her face. Abel grinned as he glanced over at the hospital bed. Blonde hair curled messily around her shoulders and a stray strand sighed up and down as she snored. Harley.

"How...?" Abel wondered.

"After you left that day, I pulled a few strings and had her transported here," Sarah explained. "She was in a coma for a while with a few complications. After she woke up, she was kept here for other health reasons, but she's finally ready to be discharged from the hospital. I didn't tell you because I didn't want to get your hopes up just to have them smashed again. Plus, you were so busy with the war."

Abel felt like jumping, dancing, screaming, and crying all at once. He looked back over at the bed and Harley opened her eyes groggily. Brilliant blue pierced Abel and he sighed. He thought he'd never be able to see that again. Harley grinned with her eyes slightly squinted.

"What're you doing all the way over there, dummy?" she croaked.

Before Abel knew what he was doing, he had crossed the room and pressed his lips to hers, savoring the moment that he thought would never come. When he finally pulled away, Harley was laughing with a twinkle in her eyes. She pulled Abel's ear next to her lips and whispered with her breath tickling his ear, "I love you, too."

Abel jerked away. "You heard that?"

Harley smirked. "I hear everything."

Abel shook his head. She hadn't changed a bit. He took a seat next to her, taking her hand in his own and talking all day until his throat was scratchy. And when it was finally dark outside, he fell asleep at her side with his hand still encasing hers. He would never let her go again.